AN ADRIAN WEST THRILLER

THE ATLANTIS CONSPIRACY

L.D. GOFFIGAN

Copyright © 2022 by L.D. Goffigan

All rights reserved.

This book or any portion thereof may not be reproduced, or stored in a retrieval system, or transmitted in any form or by any means, electronic, mechanical, photocopying, recording, or otherwise, without the express written permission of the publisher.

ldgoffiganbooks.com

This is a work of fiction. Names, characters, organizations, places, events, and incidents are either products of the author's imagination or used fictitiously.

Printed in the United States of America

Paperback ISBN: 979-8-9902344-2-0

Cover Design by Mibl Art

PROLOGUE

1200 BCE
Dikti Mountains
Crete

*P*ura watched the fires burning in the distance, desecrating the village that had once been her home.

She knew it wasn't only her village that burned; she'd heard the whispers from merchants and traders who visited other lands, both near and far. Invaders had swept onto multiple shores from the sea, either taking the lands for their own or burning them, forcing refugees to flee. She had even heard that the invaders had burned the great palatial complexes to the ground. The elders of her village said they must have displeased the gods for such misfortune to have befallen them all.

The people of her village, and others nearby, had fled to the caves in the surrounding mountains for shelter after the destruction of their homes. The leaders said they would one day return, but she feared they would never go home again.

For now, the caves were their place of refuge, where they cooked their meals over fires and slept beneath the stars when the nights were clear, where they prayed and made sacrifices to the gods, hoping that their favor would return. Though Pura was training to be a priestess, she worried the elders were right, and their prayers were for naught. They had somehow displeased the gods, and the gods had abandoned them.

Pura turned away from the sight of her burning village, retreating into the caves, moving past those who'd set up their fires for the night, who huddled together to keep warm against the upcoming chill that nightfall would bring. Unlike the other refugees, Pura had no family. Her parents had died long ago from sickness when she was still a girl. The village priestess, Kitane, had taken her in, raising her as her own while teaching her the ways of the priestesses, telling her she would one day take her place.

Pura kept going until she reached the rear of the cave, taking a narrow tunnel that was forbidden to all—to all except for Pura. The tunnel grew dark around her as she made her way farther down it; she had to use the firelight that danced at the very end to guide her.

She soon emerged into a small open area, and halted at the sight that greeted her. Kitane had forbidden anyone from entering this area, designating it as a private area of worship. She had not even allowed Pura here until now, and she could see why.

Kitane had carved something into the cave wall and was kneeling before it, her head bowed in prayer. The carving was of a labyrinth, its circular pathways leading to a center with writing in linear markings that she did not recognize. She'd not yet been trained in the markings of the scribes.

"Come forward, child," Kitane said, not turning around.

Pura stepped forward. Kitane turned, giving her a smile shadowed with sorrow.

"Soon, this will no longer be our home," Kitane said. "If it had not been the invaders, it would have been the famine that sweeps over the lands. If not the famine, the shifting of the earth."

Panic flared in Pura's belly, and she shook her head. "No. There's still—"

"Our home is already lost. But there is hope." Kitane stood and took Pura's hands, tears shimmering in her dark eyes. "We have another home, one our ancestors left long ago. They left symbols like these to help guide our way back."

"Where is this home?" Pura asked.

"Its location has been lost, but it is said to be far to the east. It was a great place, even more grand than the palatial complexes that dot these lands. I believe this is happening not because we have displeased the gods, but because we are meant to go back. The labyrinths," she said, gesturing to the cave wall, "they will guide us home. The gods will listen to our pleas and show us the way. I want you to pray with me before I leave an offering, but I need you to make me a promise first."

"What?"

"I fear that I will not be here for long. The healers tell me I am ailing and that I am soon to join the gods. You will become the chief priestess here. It will be up to you to guide the villagers to their true home. You need to do this."

Pura wanted to protest that she wasn't ready, that she didn't know what all this meant. But she knew she needed to be strong. She was a woman now, soon to be priestess of what remained of her village. This was what she had trained many years for.

"What is the name of this place?" Pura asked.

Kitane took her hand and guided her to the labyrinth, placing it on the markings in the center. She closed her eyes, her voice a reverent whisper.

"Atai. It is called the land of Atai."

CHAPTER 1

Present Day
National Archaeological Museum
Athens, Greece
10:13 A.M.

Stephanos Keliades sat hunched over in his wheelchair, his eyes fluttering, making every effort to appear like the old, feeble man he wore as a disguise. The patrons who carefully averted their gazes or gave him sympathetic smiles didn't know that he was actually a fit man of thirty-two, with a toned body he maintained by fifteen-mile daily runs and a strict weight-training routine by his expensive but effective personal trainer. He had no desire to become like the flabby older men of his organization.

The woman pushing his wheelchair through

the side entrance of the museum, the entrance designated for disabled visitors, was dressed primly as a middle-aged caregiver, her usual blonde hair dyed a mousy brown, streaked with gray. She was actually Irina, his loyal colleague and occasional lover. He knew that if Irina didn't wear her disguise, the male patrons of the museum wouldn't be able to take their eyes off her. His Irina was a knockout without even trying, with her delectable curves and sharp green eyes. Her beauty was a disguise from the ruthless killer she could be.

His bodyguard, Michalis, who had entered through the main entrance, trailed them from a discreet distance of several meters. Stephanos could feel Michalis' intense gaze on the back of the gray wig he wore. Michalis wore concealer to cover the distinctive scar on his cheek, and the cargo pants and T-shirt of a tourist, an outfit which failed to disguise his muscular, deadly form. Irina had snorted at his lack of an effective disguise, but Stephanos trusted no one more than Michalis. He had been on his security detail since he was a teenager, and he had proven his loyalty to a fault.

Irina pushed his wheelchair past the sculpture collection consisting of ancient Greek and Roman sculptures, pausing for them to occasionally study individual pieces, though neither of them were paying any attention. None of the treasures here compared to what they were seeking . . . and what it would lead them to. A place that his organization—and humanity—had sought for millennia.

They gradually made their way through the temporary exhibitions featuring pieces centering on Greek mythology, until they reached the doors to one of the conference rooms, where Irina pretended to consult her map of the museum.

The hum of anticipation coursed through Stephanos as his eyes strayed to a clock on the wall. *Almost time.* He performed the countdown in his mind.

Five ... four ... three ... two ...

The sound of a loud explosion boomed from just outside the entrance of the museum, followed by two others.

As he'd predicted, chaos ensued. Museum patrons screamed, fleeing toward the exits. Irina sprang into action, pushing his chair into the nearest men's restroom. It was thankfully empty, and with the chaos surrounding the explosions, he knew it would remain so. Michalis hurried in behind them.

Stephanos stood, stripping down to the security guard uniform he wore beneath his plaid shirt and brown pants, yanking off his wig and glasses, though he kept on the facial prothesis. He couldn't risk someone recognizing his face.

Next to him, Michalis and Irina had also stripped down to their own security guard uniforms, though it looked far sexier on Irina. He averted his gaze, ignoring the lust that shot through him at the sight. He would enjoy her body later. Now was not the time.

"Ready, my *ómorfe?*" she asked, her eyes flashing with mischief.

He leaned down and pressed his lips to hers. "Ready, *foniá.*"

He nodded at Michalis, and together, they exited the restroom. The panicked patrons were still fleeing. Stephanos, Irina, and Michalis played their parts, urging the patrons to hurry and pointing them toward the exits. Not that they needed to. It was practically a stampede as the tourists fled, a stampede that was easy for himself, Irina, and Michalis to blend into, making their way toward the rear of the museum that led to the conservation laboratory downstairs. Stephanos used the key card they'd bribed an actual security guard for, allowing them to slip inside the stairwell.

The corridor that led to the lab had already been evacuated. Stephanos made his way down the corridor, with Irina and Michalis flanking him. He knew exactly where he was going. He'd studied the floor plan of this section many times over.

They made a sharp left at the end of the corridor, Stephanos using the key card to enter the empty conservation lab.

The lab was climate-controlled, as was necessary to preserve ancient papyri. His eyes swept over the room until he spotted it. On the center long table, covered in protective plexiglass, edged by an aluminum frame, was the papyrus they'd come for.

Stephanos approached it, awe sweeping over him as he took it in. The papyrus was in fragments, but the ancient Greek written there was legible. They were words that would lead to the greatest discovery humanity would ever make. A discovery that would force humanity out of its stagnation and forward . . . to a new beginning.

"Stephanos," Irina said. Her tone was gentle but urgent. Stephanos forced himself out of his awestruck stupor and carefully lifted the plexiglass, placing it into the protective case Irina had stowed in her backpack.

Irina met his eyes and gave him a small smile. She knew how important this papyrus was to him, their organization . . . the world. He returned her smile as they exited the lab, making their way swiftly toward the rear exit door.

"Na stamatisei!"

Stephanos whirled, fury coursing through him. Two actual security guards were dashing toward them from the other end of the corridor. His hand moved to his weapon, ready to take care of the two pests. But Michalis and Irina had already taken out their weapons, easily dispatching the two guards with two perfectly aimed shots.

Stephanos turned and raced out of the exit, Michalis and Irina on his heels. Thanks to their preparations, this back alley was empty, save for the black car that awaited them.

They entered, and his driver pulled the car away from the exit. It made its way down the alley before merging into traffic on the main road in front of the museum.

As Irina and Michalis kept careful watch out of the side and rear windows, Stephanos ached to pull out the papyrus, to run his hands reverently over the words beneath the protective casing, but he couldn't risk any deterioration of the precious document. This papyrus was the key to the place he sought.

A lost city. A lost world.

Atlantis.

CHAPTER 2

FBI Headquarters
Relics and Antiquities Task Force
Washington, DC
1:27 P.M.

Adrian West's eyes roamed eagerly over the screen. She couldn't stop herself from running her hand along the letters of the ancient papyrus on the monitor. Even though it was just an image, she could almost feel the delicate material beneath her hands. Her historian brain, which she never could completely shut off, was in awe at the sight of such a rare, ancient document.

"When I get married," Vince Farinelli's wry voice said from behind her, "I want my wife to look at me the way you're looking at that old piece of paper."

Adrian turned, offering him a grin. She'd been

so caught up in the document on the large computer screen before her, she'd nearly forgotten there were several other people in the conference room. She met the gaze of her partner, Nick Harper, who was used to her fawning over ancient documents.

"Welcome to my world," Nick said to Vince, before giving her a wink. "To be fair, though, I doubt anyone would look at you that way."

Vince scowled as the others in the room chuckled. The newly formed Relics and Antiquities Task Force was only days old, but the group was quickly creating their own camaraderie.

Just a couple of weeks ago, Nick's boss at the FBI, Jeremy Briggs, had offered Adrian and Nick the opportunity to lead a specialized task force that would tackle terror threats related to stolen artifacts all over the world. The offer came after their recent successes in locating and stopping terrorists from obtaining and using artifacts to cause worldwide destruction in both Egypt and Russia. They had agreed, even though Adrian had only recently decided to return to law enforcement full time after a long stint in academia. Her recent experiences in the field had proven that this world was where she truly belonged. Briggs had fast-tracked her reinstatement to the FBI, and she was now officially part of both the bureau and this task force, which was a product of three federal agencies working together: the Department of Homeland Security, the CIA, and the FBI.

The task force was small and specialized, at least for now, Briggs had told them, hinting that the government would expand—or dismiss—the task force, depending on its results. It consisted of Vince, a tech whiz, whom Adrian had worked with before. The others were Layla Kumar, a former translator for the CIA, who specialized in ancient history and linguistics; Jonathan Harris, another tech whiz, who had also come their way from the CIA; and Sloane Carpenter, an art history and antiquities expert, formerly of FBI's Art Crimes unit and a previous coworker of Nick's during his time working there. The team was assembled to back up Adrian and Nick while they were in the field.

Adrian had worried how the other members of the task force would take to her as one of the leads, given that she'd only recently been reinstated, but Briggs assured her she was admired by the team, both because of her recent successes and her history with the bureau. Briggs seemed to be right so far. The team was friendly and professional. Given her history with the bureau, when she'd butted heads with colleagues and higher-ups, Adrian found this an immense relief.

"And this is more than just an old piece of paper, Vince," Adrian playfully scolded.

The papyrus on the screen before them had been uncovered at an archaeological site just outside of Athens several weeks ago. Its discovery pointed to the existence of a place many historians had dismissed as myth ... Atlantis.

"Refresh my memory," Vince said. "Why is this papyrus so significant?"

"I swear you don't pay attention to any of the briefings," Layla huffed. "This 'old piece of paper' is the only record outside of Plato that refers to a historical Atlantis. This papyrus is written in the hand of Solon, a historical person who Plato quoted in his writings about Atlantis."

Vince let out a low whistle, his gaze returning to the papyrus. Another surge of awe coursed through Adrian as she also took it in. Many people didn't realize that outside of Plato's dialogues *Timaeus* and *Critias*, there were no other recorded references to Atlantis. All the tales of Atlantis had been based on rather scant sources, hence the assumption that it was a fiction created by Plato. Having another recorded reference to Atlantis by a historical person was beyond significant.

The papyrus was written in ancient Greek, and heavily fragmented, but a team of paleographers had pieced together some of the crucial words.

> SEEK PROOF OF THIS GREAT CIVILIZA-
> TION CALLED ATLANTIS, ATAI IN THE OLD
> TONGUE, ATAI IN THE OLD WRITING, AND
> THE MARKERS FOR ITS FALL. I WILL SAIL
> TO SEE IT WITH MY OWN EYES, FOR IT
> WILL HELP STRENGTHEN ATHENS AND STOP
> TYRANTS FROM

It was only a fragmented couple of sentences, but those few words said so much. The word that Solon referred to, Atai, was determined by linguists to be a pre-Greek word for Atlantis. He'd also written the word Atai in the Linear A script, an undeciphered writing system from the ancient Minoan civilization, which had helped linguists partially decipher some parts of the script.

Law enforcement agencies had miraculously kept the discovery under wraps thus far. The law agencies who were monitoring the threats around the find had mutually agreed to not release it to the press yet, and only a select few curators, linguists, and historians knew about it. She and Nick were flying out that evening to Athens to see the papyrus in person and assist the local authorities there with any leads that could point to the actual Atlantis, putting them ahead of the dangerous groups with ties to terrorism that international law enforcement agencies were watching to prevent them from getting to it first. Though she knew the journey ahead would be dangerous, the historian in her was brimming with excitement at the prospect of finding an actual historical Atlantis.

Briggs entered the conference room, his mouth set in a grim line. Adrian stiffened at the sight of his hard expression. Something was wrong.

"I need you and Nick to leave immediately," Briggs said without preamble. "There's been an explosion at the National Archaeological Museum in Athens. Someone's stolen the papyrus."

L.D. GOFFIGAN

CHAPTER 3

National Archaeological Museum
Athens, Greece
10:15 A.M.

Adrian and Nick trailed Lieutenant Constable Athena Karras through the main gallery of the National Archaeological Museum. The museum was one of Adrian's favorites; she had visited over a dozen times, most recently during an academic conference several years before. It featured a treasure trove of priceless Greek antiquities.

But Adrian didn't have time to admire the ancient treasures that surrounded them. Athena, who insisted they call her by her first name, was an imposing woman, nearly as tall as Nick, with a mane of dark curls and sharply intelligent amber eyes. She was guiding them through the museum, retracing the same path the thieves had taken.

"They entered through the side entrance—we believe they were in disguise. The explosions were set off remotely, caused by simple pressure bombs hidden just outside the entrance. Fortunately, there were no fatalities, just some injuries. We don't believe they intended to kill. They wanted to create a distraction. After the explosions, they made their way down to the conservation lab using a key card they bribed or stole from a guard," Athena said, guiding them through the main gallery of the museum as she spoke.

She led them to the rear of the main gallery and into a stairwell, where she pointed up at a security camera. "This camera was shut off. They managed to hack into the security camera system—we're still trying to figure out exactly how they did that. From here, we surmised they made their way into the conservation lab, stole the papyrus, then made their way out of the back exit before making their escape."

Adrian nodded, considering her words. The thieves had carefully planned and executed the theft. She ran a quick mental profile of the thieves. *Sophisticated, possessing resources or wealth, efficient.*

"We've been interviewing employees, especially the security personnel," Athena continued.

"Anything significant yet?" Nick asked.

"No," Athena said, and Adrian could see the frustration in her eyes. "But we're still working our way through the interviews."

"We'd like to see the transcripts—or video of the interviews, if possible," Nick said.

"Of course," Athena said, giving him a polite nod.

Adrian was relieved that Athena didn't seem to resent their presence here, as was often the case when multiple law enforcement agencies were on a single case. On the contrary, Athena seemed relieved when they arrived and grateful for outside assistance.

Athena's phone shrilled, and she gave them an apologetic look before stepping away to take the call.

"What are you thinking?" Nick asked.

"A highly sophisticated team with a great deal of resources," Adrian said. "Professionals, through and through."

"Agreed. In Art Crimes we only saw these types of heists for high-profile items in the millions."

"This is hardly a twenty-million-dollar painting," Adrian countered. "The papyrus is invaluable, but it's too rare and easily trackable to be sold on the black market or to a private buyer."

"They don't intend to sell it, then," Nick said, thinking out loud. "They could be using it to find Atlantis. Which begs the question—how did they even know about it? The find's been kept under wraps."

"There's obviously been a leak somewhere," Adrian said grimly. "I want to know . . . why take the risk to steal it? A team with their resources could easily get access to an electronic version of the papyrus."

Before Nick could respond, Athena returned, her brow furrowed as she gave Adrian a quizzical look.

"That was the local hospital. A curator who works here and was injured in the explosion is awake . . . and he asked specifically for you, Adrian."

Center of Historical and Scientific Research
Athens, Greece
10:47 A.M.

THE CENTER OF HISTORICAL and Scientific Research, CHSR, was located on the outskirts of Athens. A private research facility that wove into all areas of the sciences, its main campus was in Athens but had branches all over the world. The Athens campus buildings were stonewashed white to mimic the ancient buildings that once dotted the city, with the main building bearing the logo of the Phaistos Disc, a Minoan artifact dotted with mysterious symbols that had never been deciphered, and was meant to stand for untapped knowledge, knowledge that CHSR was established to uncover.

It had expanded greatly in the nearly two centuries since its founding, thanks to generous endowments from wealthy benefactors, as well as funding from the select few who knew its true purpose.

Stephanos made his way down the spacious corridor of the main building, entering the conference room that looked out over the glittering waters of the Saronic Gulf, irritation coursing through him. Several men and women, board members of CHSR, sat around the large oak table. They gave him icy glares as he stepped inside the room.

Stephanos gritted his teeth but forced a polite smile. He should be sitting at the head of the table as his father had once, rather than summoned like an errant child. Given that he was decades younger than the people glaring at him, that was exactly what it felt like.

"Do you realize what risk you put yourself in by your actions at the museum? The risk you put this organization in?" Dmitris Karagiannis hissed.

Dmitris was an austere man in his late fifties; he'd been a close friend of his father's but had seemed to never like Stephanos. Still, Stephanos was surprised by the older man's vitriol. He'd been prepared for the others to be . . . annoyed by his participation in the heist, but not to this level.

"Do you realize what would have happened if you'd been caught?" Zacharias, Dmitris' sour-faced son, who sat next to Dmitris, demanded, his face red with anger. Zacharias was younger than him by several years, but like his father, acted like he was much older—and superior to—Stephanos.

"I didn't get caught," Stephanos snapped, his temper taking hold of him. He closed his eyes, taking in several deep breaths. His late mother was fond of reminding him that he'd inherited his father's temper. He took another breath before continuing. "I chose to undertake the task myself—along with two trusted colleagues—because I knew I could handle it, and frankly I didn't trust anyone else."

The board members bristled at his words, but Stephanos evenly held their gazes.

"Are you saying you don't trust us?" Dmitris returned.

"I'm saying that I handled the job. We have the papyrus in hand. All this talk of how it was acquired is a waste of time. The authorities are already looking. I have safeguards in place that will buy us time, but that won't last forever."

They still glared at him, but he knew his words had penetrated.

"Now that you have the papyrus, have you made any headway?" Dmitris asked.

"I have a team working on it now."

"Where is this team?" asked Phillip Giorgios, a heavyset man with crow-like features, his eyes dark as they settled on Stephanos.

"I'd rather keep that knowledge to myself for now."

Stephanos could practically see steam coming from their ears at his words. Dmitris leaned forward, his face tight with anger.

"You—" he sputtered.

"Given the high level of interest in the papyrus by international law enforcement, I think it's all in our best interest to keep its location secret for now. If any of you are questioned, you won't have any knowledge to incriminate yourselves or this operation," Stephanos coolly interrupted.

A heavy, tense silence fell over the room. Once again, he knew his words had penetrated.

"You have two days," Dmitris snapped. "Two days, and then we want to know where this team is, who they consist of, and what they've learned. Despite what you seem to think, this is not your operation alone."

It should be, he wanted to snarl. It was his great-great-grandfather who'd founded CHSR, and then passed its knowledge, and true purpose, to his son, and down the family line, until it reached him. He was one of the few who'd taken the knowledge seriously and had planned for years what he would do with it. As far as Stephanos was concerned, the board members who weren't on his side were dead weight. He had true allies in the organization, and it was only their opinion that mattered.

But he needed all the leaders and their resources . . . for now. Once he had what he wanted, they would be of no importance. He looked forward to the day that he would eliminate them. Perhaps he would do the deed himself.

At the thought, he gave them a smile that was genuine.

"Of course," he said simply.

Without waiting for their dismissal, he turned to leave the room. Once he found what he sought and carried out his plans, none of their petty concerns would matter. *They* wouldn't matter. The world would be forever changed, and he would have the ultimate power he craved.

CHAPTER 4

Palinisos General Hospital
Athens, Greece
11:30 AM

Adrian, Nick, and Athena approached Elias Mandreou's hospital room. They entered to find a brunette man in his thirties who had the look of a disheveled professor. He hastily sat up when they entered, reaching for his glasses on the side table.

After Athena introduced them, Elias' eyes swept over the three of them.

"I want to talk to Agent West alone," he said.

Athena looked irritated, but left the room without argument. Adrian shook her head when Nick also started to leave, reaching out to take his arm.

"Nick is my partner, and he stays," she said firmly.

Elias looked as if he were going to argue for a moment, but seemed to decide against it, giving her a grudging nod.

"It's an honor to meet you, Agent West. I read everything I could about the Cleopatra discovery, which led me to your other academic work. I loved your paper on the potential linguistic origins of the Polynesian language families."

Adrian gave him a polite smile, but studied him closely. He seemed on edge. He couldn't have asked to see her just to compliment her on an old academic paper she wrote. "Thank you. Why did you want to see me?" she asked, deciding it was best to get right to the point.

"I wanted to offer my expertise in case there was anything I could help with."

"OK," Adrian said slowly. Something told her he wasn't being completely truthful. "Right now, we're just trying to find any information we can on the thieves. Did you witness anything before, during, or after the explosion?"

"I got knocked out during the first explosion, so I'm afraid there's not much I can help you with as a witness." He gestured to his arm, wincing as he lifted it. "I sprained my arm when I fell and gave myself a light concussion."

"Then what—" Nick began, but he faltered as Elias pressed his finger to his lips, handing Adrian his phone.

Adrian took it, freezing at the message that was typed in large letters in a text:

> I have another possible lead on the location of Atlantis—an inscription. I can't risk the police outside overhearing. I will tell you why later. Please play along for now.

She met his gaze. There was a quiet urgency in their depths.

A million questions raced through her mind. She had thought that law enforcement had kept the Solon papyrus under wraps, but the thieves knew about it, as did this curator. And what was this other lead he was referring to? Was it genuine, or was he just a hanger-on who wanted to insert himself into the case?

Adrian handed the phone to Nick, who read the message.

"What exactly is the nature of your expertise?" she asked Elias, keeping her tone neutral, though her heart was racing.

"Well, my background is—" Elias began, but the sound of shouts and screams interrupted him from outside, followed by two gunshots. The sounds came from the far end of the corridor.

Adrian and Nick whirled. She moved to the door, cracking it open and peering out.

Her heart plummeted in her chest. Athena was nowhere to be seen, and two armed men approached Elias' hotel room with deadly purpose.

CHAPTER 5

Adrian took out her service weapon, locking the door as Nick rushed forward to barricade it.

"Two armed men heading right this way," she said to Nick, who gave her a quick nod.

Adrian whirled to face Elias, who had stumbled out of bed, trembling with fear. Her gut told her that whoever had breached the hospital was after him, and revolved around what he wanted to tell her.

"Can you run?" she asked, approaching him.

"I don't think I have a choice," he shakily replied.

He was right. They needed to get out of there, and fast. Adrian helped him away from his bed, Nick moving to her side to help. Together, they made their way over to the window. Adrian uttered a silent prayer of gratitude that they were on the first floor.

Just outside of the hospital room, Adrian heard several grunts and the sound of a scuffle. She hurried forward, yanking open the window, and they both helped Elias out.

Another gunshot sounded, perilously close to the door. Moving quickly, Adrian climbed out after Elias, followed by Nick, just as the door to the hospital room burst open—

A tall and broad-shouldered man entered, his gaze landing on them. Nick raised his sidearm, firing off two shots. The man crumpled to the ground, but more footsteps were approaching.

Adrian hooked her arm around Elias and helped him away from the window.

"Keep low!" Adrian shouted. They moved down into a crouch, scrambling away from the window and toward the parking lot. Nick flanked her and Elias from the rear, his weapon out.

A gunshot rang through the air, perilously close to Adrian's side. Nick fired back, and Adrian gripped Elias, who was unsteady on his feet.

"Elias—we have to run," she said.

Elias nodded, and together, they raced toward Adrian and Nick's rental car.

Adrian helped him inside, with Elias cradling his injured arm as she dove into the driver's seat, Nick hurrying in after her. Another man darted through the parking lot toward them, raising his weapon to shoot, but Adrian had already fired up the ignition.

"Get down!" she shouted to Nick and Elias, flooring the accelerator and peeling out of the parking lot as shots rang out in their wake.

CHAPTER 6

*A*drian sped through the streets away from the hospital, weaving in and out of traffic, ignoring the irritated horns of other drivers. Her eyes flew periodically to the rearview mirror for any sign of a pursuer, her heart hammering, but so far, they seemed to be in the clear.

At her side, Elias was tense and silent, his grip white-knuckled on his knees. Nick sat in the back seat, his service weapon out and at the ready, scanning the surrounding streets.

Adrian gradually slowed down her speed, merging in with other traffic and not stopping until they reached the Psyrri neighborhood, an area filled with a maze of winding streets decorated with hip street art and modern shops, a sharp contrast to the ancient buildings that dotted Athens. She parked on a small street in front of graffiti that read, in Greek, the Hippocrates' quote: *Life is short and art is long.* In the distance, she could make out the gleaming marble structure of the Parthenon, proudly perched on the hill of the acropolis.

She cut the engine and turned to face Elias, adrenaline still humming through her veins.

"Those men were looking for you," she stated. "I'm going to take a guess that it has to do with this inscription you mentioned. What exactly is your area of expertise?"

"Ancient Mediterranean civilizations," he replied. He closed his eyes briefly, pressing his head back against his seat. "I don't know how they knew about it. My contact—he only told me about it. He knows what a valuable find it is."

"Do you trust him?" Adrian asked. "Because those men—"

"Absolutely," Elias said. "He's incredibly careful with his finds. He only came to me because he needed my expertise to confirm its authenticity."

Adrian studied him. There were no obvious tells that he was lying, but she couldn't shake the feeling that he wasn't being fully truthful with her.

"Why did you want to tell me about this?" Adrian pressed. "Why not immediately go to the authorities?"

Elias didn't answer right away, shifting uncomfortably in his seat. Nick leaned forward, his patience wearing thin. "Given what's just happened, we're your best friends right now. Talk."

"I don't trust the local police," he said. "And neither does my contact."

Adrian drummed her fingers on the steering wheel. Why would they not trust the local police?

And then understanding dawned.

"Elias," Adrian said carefully. "Is the method your contact used to find this inscription... legal?"

Elias' silence was the only answer she needed, and she detected a hint of shame in his eyes. Nick let out a muffled curse.

It was increasingly clear that Elias' contact was operating on the antiquities black market or had obtained the artifact through illegal means. Adrian exchanged a look with Nick, whose mouth was set in a grim line. She knew Nick was familiar with such types because of his work with the FBI's Art Crimes department, and he didn't look thrilled at the prospect of having to rely on a black-market dealer. This explained his caginess, and his contact not wanting to go to the police.

Still, Adrian wondered why he'd come to her with this, especially when she and Nick could take him in for obtaining such information illegally. There was something else he was hiding; she just couldn't pinpoint it. Something just wasn't adding up.

"How about this?" Nick asked Elias, his tone turning hard. "We take you to the FBI office here, and you can tell them about—"

"Nick," Adrian interrupted, holding up her hand. As suspicious as she was of Elias, he had information valuable enough for someone to come after him for it. She turned back to Elias, who had gone pale at Nick's words. "What else can you tell us?"

"My contact wouldn't tell me where he found the inscription. He just showed me an image."

Adrian jumped as a loud boom abruptly sounded in the near distance as a car backfired, and another car zipped past them. Her pulse raced, and she tightened her grip on the steering wheel.

"We need to get out of the open and see this inscription," she said.

"I have it stored in an encrypted file and can't access it on my phone. I need to get to a computer. I know somewhere safe we can go for the time being," Elias said. "A cousin of mine has a home in Marousi—it's just outside of Athens."

"How do we know the men looking for you won't search there?" Nick demanded.

Though still pale, Elias gave him a wry smile. "You don't understand Greek families, my friend. I have scores of cousins."

Adrian eyed him, heaving a sigh. They needed to get off the road and, for the time being, take Elias' word for it that this place in Marousi was safe.

"Tell us how to get there."

Marousi, Greece
2:15 P.M.

MAROUSI WAS LOCATED to the northeast of Athens. One of the great cities during the age of the Athenian Republic, its name derived from that of a hunter of the Greek goddess Artemis, Amarysia. Now, it was a bustling, modern suburb, and Adrian had to maneuver through heavy midday traffic to arrive in the quiet neighborhood, where Elias' cousin's home was located.

The home they arrived at was a modest Mediterranean-style, single-level home tucked away at the end of a narrow street. Looking around before they got out of the car, Adrian and Nick escorted Elias to the front door, which he unlocked with a key hidden at the base of a plant pot.

Once Adrian and Nick confirmed the home was empty, Elias made his way to a couch in the living room, while Nick gave him a bottle of water from the fridge in the adjoining kitchen. Elias took it with gratitude, taking a large swig.

"How's your arm?" Adrian asked.

"Still sore, but nothing painkillers can't help. The doctors were planning on releasing me today," Elias said. "I just wasn't expecting to literally have to run for my life."

He gulped more water down before directing them to a laptop stowed away in a desk drawer in the corner of the living room. Adrian grabbed it and handed it to him. Elias typed something on the screen before turning it to face Adrian and Nick.

They took it in. The image was of a clay shard inscribed with linear markings that Adrian recognized as the Linear A script. She stilled at the sight of the markings, which changed this from an ordinary ancient artifact to something extraordinary.

It was the pre-Greek word for Atlantis . . . the same one found on Solon's papyrus.

CHAPTER 7

Athens, Greece
3:06 P.M.

Athena Karras awoke in a haze of disorientation. She blinked, looking round the hospital room, uncertain how she'd gotten here.

And then it all came back to her. The armed men striding toward her as she turned the corner, on her way to grab a coffee to give Elias privacy with the two American agents. One of them raising his weapon to fire. The flash of pain. Blackness.

"Hey."

Athena jumped as her colleague, Stavros Vlachis, entered, clutching a cup of tea in his hands. His eyes were heavy with fatigue, but she saw relief fill them as he approached her bedside. "Welcome to the land of the living."

Athena started to sit up, wincing at the sudden sharp spike of pain in her shoulder.

"Easy," Stavros said, setting down his tea. "You just took a bullet to the shoulder. Doctors say it was lucky you were wearing your vest. If you weren't . . ." He trailed off, pain twisting his features.

Athena lifted up her hand, and he took it, squeezing it in his own. She gave him a reassuring smile. She knew how much her partner cared about her. They had always been close, to the point where she knew that some of their coworkers thought they were having an affair. Impossible, considering how devoted Stavros was to his wife, Helena, and Athena's complete lack of attraction to men. The bond they shared was more like brother and sister.

"Hey," she said, winking. "I'm not that easy to kill."

He returned her smile. Athena leaned back against the pillows, even though she desperately wanted to get up. She just didn't feel like arguing with her overprotective partner.

"What do we have?" she asked. "Any leads on who those men were?"

"We're examining security camera footage now. There were two of them. They entered right through the front doors, knocking out the security guard who tried to stop them. They made their way right to Elias' room, so it was definitely him they were after. After they got past you, they made it into Elias' room, but the American agents got Elias out."

"Do we know where they are?"

"We're doing a search, already in contact with their higher-ups and the FBI office here in Athens. But no one's heard anything yet."

"They probably don't trust us," Athena said. Those men had known exactly where to find Elias. An uneasy shiver went down her spine. What if someone in their department been compromised?

"Yeah. I wouldn't blame them," Stavros muttered.

Athena studied him. On second glance, there was more than just fatigue and worry in his eyes . . . there was anxiety as well.

"Stavros?" she asked carefully. "What's going on?"

Stavros looked at her for a long moment, as if he wanted to say something, but seemed to decide against it. "Just trying to put together all the pieces of the puzzle. But I'm on it," Stavros said, giving her a look of reassurance. "You just get your rest. You'll be fine, but the doctors want to keep you overnight."

Athena stared at him for a long moment. She knew her partner—her friend—and he was definitely hiding something. "Stavros—"

"I have to get back to the station. Just wanted to check on my favorite partner. I'll give you more updates as I get them."

Before Athena could reply, he leaned over to give her a quick peck on the cheek, then hurried out of the hospital room.

Athena watched him go, baffled. What was

Stavros hiding? Was it related to who had sent those men after Elias? To the stolen papyrus?

She was determined to find out.

~

Marousi, Greece
3:15 P.M.

Adrian and Nick took in the inscription in awed silence. A *second* reference to Atlantis outside of Plato? No wonder Elias' contact was cagey. Such a find was priceless.

Her eyes moved to the other words, frustration filling her. Not only could she not decipher the markings, but it appeared the camera was zoomed in on the image, cutting off the rest of the markings.

"Are there any more images?" Adrian asked.

"My contact keeps his finds close to the vest. That's the only part of the inscription he was willing to show me. If I want to see the whole thing, he'd have to show it to me in person."

"That's convenient," Nick said drily.

"It's his way of being careful," Elias returned, a defensive edge to his tone.

"How did your contact know about the word for Atlantis in pre-Greek—especially written in Linear A? The discovery of the papyrus has been kept under wraps," Adrian asked.

"I didn't tell him about the papyrus. He must

have found out about it some other way. Like I said before, I think he just wanted my confirmation."

Adrian's eyes returned to the markings. She was well aware of, and fascinated by, the Linear A script, as were many historical linguists, given that it was one of the few still undeciphered writing systems from the ancient world. Clay tablets of Linear A had been found all over Crete, the Aegean, Greece, the Levant, and Asia Minor. No one knew for certain what language Linear A was supposed to depict, but it was generally assumed that it was a Minoan language, or languages, as little was known about the Minoan language itself. Even the ancient Greeks hadn't been able to decipher Linear A. It was another reason the Solon papyrus find was extraordinary. It provided linguists with some means to decrypt it, which they'd been working on since its discovery.

"This is why I wanted to talk to you," Elias said. "I know you're a talented historical linguist—it's a skill set I don't have. I thought you might be able to decipher at least one of these other markings."

Adrian tore her eyes away from the image on the screen to study Elias, wary. She was still suspicious as to why he'd reached out to her. Surely a curator would know other historical linguists, or even one of the linguists currently working to decrypt Linear A, based on the discovery of Solon's papyrus. She still had the nagging sense that he was hiding something.

Despite her suspicion, she considered his words. She could use the Linear B script to help decipher the inscription. The Linear B script was a descendant of Linear A that had been successfully deciphered back in the 1950s. It was determined that it was an early form of Greek, its alphabet predating the Greek alphabet by centuries. It was used by the Mycenaean civilization, a civilization that arose after the Minoan one fell. When the Mycenaean civilization also ended, sending the Greek isles into a time historians called the Greek Dark Ages, it fell out of use. The little that was known about Linear A was all due to Linear B.

Still, she doubted she could single-handedly decipher a script that countless other linguists had been attempting to for decades. She at least needed to see more of the inscription to determine exactly what she was working with. And then she'd have to reach out to the team in DC to get their help with a potential partial decipherment.

She turned to Nick, who, as always, seemed to know what she was going to say. He let out a heavy sigh and gave her a nod.

"I'll need to see more of the inscription first," she said. "Take us to your contact."

CHAPTER 8

Athens, Greece
4:02 P.M.

Stephanos hovered over his handpicked team of paleographists, glaring down at them with impatience. They were gathered over the Solon papyrus, studying every inch carefully through the protective glass that covered it.

He knew his presence was distracting them, but he didn't care. He had set up a state-of-the-art conservation lab in the basement of his villa that could rival any of the world's top museums, complete with temperature, humidity and light controls, along with the latest 3D scanning equipment and computers. Still, they had made no progress.

"Have you found anything yet?" he asked shortly.

One paleographist, a young Italian woman,

Gabriella, seemed to be the only one brave enough to look up at him while the others remained huddled over the papyrus.

"Right now, there's no indication that there's anything other than the writing referring to Atlantis," she said tentatively. "Are you certain that there's—"

"Yes," he snapped. "Keep looking. You have all the tools and resources at your disposal. Time is of the essence."

Gabriella dutifully bowed her head and resumed her work. Stephanos' eyes slid to the delicate papyrus, a sliver of unease filling him. What if there was nothing more to the papyrus?

But he shook the thought away. Though he had another lead that more of his experts were working on, this would be the most likely path to lead him directly to Atlantis.

He turned to the doorway of the lab, where Irina hovered, her arms crossed, her features tight with disapproval. She had urged him to let his team do his work, that it would take time. He had curtly told her not to tell him how to lead his team. He gritted his teeth as he met her disapproving gaze; despite her beauty, talents in bed, and the lethality which had attracted him to her in the first place, he was starting to find her irritating.

Stephanos approached her, keeping his expression hard.

"Has Elias Mandreou been found yet?" he asked.

"He's still missing, along with those two American agents. But we're searching. We'll find them."

He closed his eyes, expelling a sharp breath. Things were not going to plan. He felt a pressure on his arm and looked up. Irina's expression had softened, and she was stroking his arm.

"Calm down, *agapi mou*," she murmured, using the same seductive tone she used in bed, which did nothing to calm him and only irritated him more. "Things will progress. We just—"

He captured her arm, clutching it in a firm grip so hard that she winced. "You don't give me orders or tell me to calm down. Just because I've had you in my bed does not mean you're my equal." He abruptly released her, and she stumbled back, her face pale. "I'll be in my wing. I expect an immediate update on any progress."

He left, not waiting for her response, but he didn't miss the flash of anger in her sharp green eyes. He didn't care; she needed to be reminded of her place.

Stephanos took the elevator to the top floor of his sprawling villa, keeping deep breaths to maintain his calm, to quell his rising frustration. Comprising of three pools—two outdoor, one indoor; a spa; all-white interiors filled with modern, designer furniture; and floor-to-ceiling glass windows that flooded the rooms with Greece's natural sunlight, his villa was his sanctuary. Lush gardens and high gates surrounded the villa, guarded by his personal security team.

The top floor was his own personal wing. It consisted of his massive bedroom, an office, meditation room, and a Turkish-style spa. When he reached his wing, he immediately made his way to his meditation room, sinking down onto the lush pillows in the center of the room.

His meditation room was where he allowed the knowledge of the ancient wisdom to course through him. He didn't worship the old gods like many members of the organization, nor did he take part in their silly rituals or offerings. He preferred to read the works of the greats, those who were believed to be founding members of the secret society that would lead to CHSR . . . those who wished to find Atlantis.

He thought of one of his favorite quotes, from the philosopher Heraclitus. *War is father of all and king of all, and some he manifested as gods, some as men; some he made slaves, some free.*

Beautiful words that described the tension of opposites that created harmony. Destruction leading to creation. That was what he intended to do.

CHSR was the modern iteration of an ancient, secret society, *Archaia Sofia,* which translated to ancient wisdom. Dating to the time of the ancient Greeks, it prized wisdom over all else. Even Plato himself was rumored to have been a member.

The board members of CHSR were nothing like the ancients; they didn't have the courage to do what needed to be done. They thought he was searching for Atlantis to seek its treasures to enrich their organization. There were only a handful who knew about his true plans, including Irina and Michalis. They knew of the sacrifices that needed to be made to start the world anew.

The key to the destruction necessary to create a new world . . . it all lay with Atlantis. He would be the one to find it. The one who would start a new world.

CHAPTER 9

Heraklion, Crete
7:12 P.M.

Adrian took in the sights of the colorful buildings that dotted Heraklion as Elias navigated their rental car through the streets.

Heraklion, the largest city on the island of Crete, was a port city that overlooked the Gulf of Heraklion. Though it was now filled with colorful modern buildings, much of its architecture indicated its ancient past. The city had been under the control of many powers over the centuries after the fall of the Minoan civilization, which had once dominated Crete, from the Byzantines, Venetians to the Ottomans. These powers had left behind many structures—from the fortifications built by the Byzantines to the Koules Fortress, built by the Venetians. The even more ancient Bronze Age palace of Knossos, a major building left behind by the Minoan civilization, lay just to the south of the city that attracted much of Crete's tourism.

With the help of the task force back in DC, whom they had updated on their whereabouts and their escape from the hospital with Elias, they had gotten a same-day flight to Crete, which was a short one-hour flight from Athens.

Adrian had been wary when Elias told her that his contact, who went by the name Socrates, didn't live in Athens.

"Socrates?" Nick muttered, with an eye roll. "Clever."

"I don't know exactly where he lives, but the address Socrates gave me is in Heraklion," Elias replied.

Nick had been even more hesitant, and Adrian had to convince him, reminding him of the significance of finding another artifact that referred to Atlantis, and its potential revelations about Atlantis' location. Given that someone had sent men after Elias, that someone had to know about the artifact as well. They needed to get to it first.

They soon arrived at a run-down apartment building in downtown Heraklion. Elias parked on a side street opposite the building, turning to face them, his expression tight.

"Let me do the talking. He knows we're coming, but he's wary of strangers. And . . . I didn't tell him you were federal agents, but historical linguists who wanted to confirm the inscription's veracity," he said.

Nick looked annoyed, but Adrian gave Elias a hasty nod of agreement. They exited the rental and approached the building, Adrian instinctively looking around to make certain no one was watching them, but none of the passersby paid them any mind.

They entered the building, making their way up three flights of stairs. Elias headed to a door at the end of the corridor and knocked, but there was no immediate answer.

Elias knocked again. Still no answer.

Adrian's instincts were immediately on alert. She and Nick exchanged a glance, reaching for their service weapons.

Adrian mouthed for Elias to step back. He swallowed and complied, moving behind her and Nick. She and Nick moved forward, and Adrian tested the door. It swung right open.

Adrian and Nick entered, weapons at the ready. The tiny one-bedroom apartment was completely trashed. Someone had torn through it.

"Socrates?" Elias shouted, entering behind them, his voice shaking with worry.

Nick gestured for him to stay behind them as he and Adrian cautiously advanced to the bedroom.

As soon as they entered, Elias stumbled back with a shocked cry.

A man lay sprawled on the floor at the foot of the bed, a gunshot wound to the center of his chest, his eyes wide and unseeing.

CHAPTER 10

Adrian knelt down by Socrates' body, examining it. The gunshot wounds to the center of his chest and just below his temple was fresh . . . he'd been killed recently.

She looked around the bedroom, her old crime scene knowledge returning to the forefront, mentally reviewing what had likely happened. Socrates had let in his attacker, and then a confrontation had taken place. She eyed the bedroom window, which led to a fire escape. Perhaps Socrates had retreated to this room, seeking an escape. The assailant had pursued him, shot him point-blank in the chest, and then shot him a second time to make certain the deed was done. He'd then trashed the apartment in search of something before leaving. She could see no sign of a phone or wallet. Both were likely taken by his killer.

She straightened. Nick was standing next to

Elias, who was pale and trembling, a comforting hand on his shoulder.

"I'm sorry, Elias," Adrian murmured. "Do you have any idea who could have done this?"

"No. His job was risky, but he was always extremely careful," Elias replied, taking a shuddering breath.

Adrian's mind ran over the possibilities. As an antiquities dealer on the black market, there was no doubt that he had enemies, but it was too much of a coincidence that he would stumble across an artifact that referred to Atlantis—only the second one in the world after the Solon papyrus—and then turn up dead. She thought about the theft in Athens and the men who'd come after Elias. This was all connected. It had to be.

She froze, a terrible thought occurring to her. Had Socrates' murderer gotten his hands on the artifact?

"He wouldn't be foolish enough to keep such a rare artifact here," Elias said, as if reading her mind. "He was very good at keeping such things hidden."

"Which is probably what his murderer was looking for," Nick said grimly.

"We need to call this in," Adrian said, heaving a sigh. "And then we need to find this artifact . . . somehow. Elias, do you—"

Adrian halted when she heard footsteps approaching the apartment. They all froze. She and Nick moved out of the bedroom, Adrian gesturing for Elias to remain behind. She and Nick crept into the living room with their service weapons drawn.

Adrian braced herself as the doorknob turned and the door opened.

A petite woman entered, her gaze hard, a pistol in her hand that she pointed right at their chests.

CHAPTER 11

"Myia, what are you doing?" Elias demanded.

Myia ignored him, keeping her pistol trained on Adrian and Nick, her sharp brown eyes never wavering. She was olive skinned with a mane of thick curly hair haphazardly tucked into a ponytail. Despite her petite stature, there was a strength to her, and Adrian got the sense that Myia could easily hold her own in a fight with someone much larger. She didn't look at all intimidated by Adrian and Nick aiming their own weapons at her.

"Who the hell are you? What are you doing in Socrates' apartment?" Myia demanded, glaring at them.

"They're friends," Elias replied, his voice shaky. "Myia, please but the gun down. Socrates . . . he's dead."

His voice wavered, and Myia paled at his

words, though her pistol remained pointed at Adrian and Nick.

"This is Adrian West and Nick Harper," Elias continued. "They're historical linguists."

Myia let out a sarcastic snort. "Please, Elias. They have law enforcement written all over them. Tell me the truth."

"You're forgetting," Nick said tightly, his eyes narrowed as he studied Myia, "that we have guns too."

"Oh, I haven't forgotten," Myia returned.

Adrian expelled a breath, placing down her weapon. Despite the other woman's suspicion, and the pistol she had leveled at them, she didn't sense imminent danger from her. This was someone who likely worked in the black market as well and didn't trust easily. She could tell Myia was a no-nonsense type, and the best way to deescalate the situation was with the truth.

"We're looking for Atlantis," Adrian said bluntly. "Socrates had an artifact that referenced it, and that's why Elias brought us here, but we found him dead. That is the truth. Now we're *all* going to lower our guns," she added, looking pointedly at Nick.

Myia stiffened at the mention of Atlantis, but she didn't look surprised. *She already knows about the papyrus*, Adrian realized. It was increasingly looking like the find wasn't as secret as she'd thought.

Still, Myia's grip on her gun didn't waver.

Adrian sized her up. She and Nick could probably take on Myia and disarm her, but they would risk her fleeing or refusing to tell them whatever she knew, and there was no doubt in her mind that Myia had some information, at the very least about Socrates and possibly the artifact. They needed her trust.

"That's not the whole truth. You're American. Feds? CIA?" Myia snapped.

"We're not answering any of your damn questions until you lower that gun," Nick snapped.

"We're not here for anything but information on Atlantis," Adrian said, holding her gaze. "In doing that, we'll find out who killed your friend. But we all have to lower our weapons first. I'm going to count to three."

Myia's mouth tightened, but she didn't protest.

"One," Adrian said, her heart hammering, praying that her instincts were right about this woman.

"Two."

Neither Myia nor Nick moved. Adrian took a breath.

"Three."

To her relief, both Nick and Myia lowered their weapons, though Myia kept hers in her hand, just pointed to the ground.

"I want to see Socrates," she said, her voice losing some of its steel.

Adrian bit her lip to hold back a protest; this apartment was now a crime scene and shouldn't be further corrupted. But by the determined look in Myia's eyes, Adrian doubted that she and Nick could stop her.

She and Nick stepped back as Myia trailed Elias to the bedroom. She heard a muffled curse, and a strangled sob. After several moments, Myia stepped back out, her face pale and stricken.

"We need to leave. This is a crime scene, and we're calling this in," Adrian said. "If you don't mind, we want to ask you questions about your friend. But we have to leave this apartment." At Myia's lingering hesitation, Adrian continued, "We're federal agents from a special task force of the FBI here to assist with finding a stolen papyrus in Athens."

Myia turned to glare at Elias. "You brought American federal agents— "

"We're not interested in you," Nick interrupted. "Just in whatever can lead us to that stolen papyrus."

"Someone killed your friend, likely because of what he knew," Adrian added. "Help us, and that will only lead to whoever killed him. And if this info leads us to Atlantis, we can talk to our superiors about a reward."

Adrian probably shouldn't have mentioned a reward. She couldn't guarantee one, but knew that this would appeal to a mercenary type like Myia. Nick looked at Adrian with raised eyebrows, but she subtly shook her head. By the look of greed and interest that flared in Myia's eyes, she could see that the tactic had worked.

"Let me see your badges," Myia said.

Adrian complied. Nick gritted his teeth but handed it over. Myia examined them before giving them an abrupt nod.

"I won't talk to the Greek police—I don't trust them. But I know a safe place we can talk. And then I want to know more about this reward."

CHAPTER 12

Heraklion, Crete
8:48 P.M.

The home Myia drove them to was a sleek, modern, split-level seafront home that overlooked the Gulf of Heraklion. Myia vaguely told them it was the home of a "friend."

Adrian and Nick had alerted the local police before looping in the team in DC, purposefully leaving out Myia's presence, at her request. Myia had done a quick sweep of the apartment, even looking into Socrates' typical hiding places, confirming that whoever killed him had taken his phone, computer and any other relevant belongings. During the drive over, Elias told them he knew Myia from a handful of archaeological digs in the surrounding Athens area. They were both evasive about exactly what Myia did; Adrian gleaned she was in the same "field" that Socrates was. She also suspected that Myia, like Socrates, wasn't her real name; Myia was the name of an ancient Greek philosopher. Adrian knew Myia was still a long way from trusting them. Adrian just needed her to trust them enough to tell them what she knew.

As soon as they stepped into the spacious foyer, Myia turned to face them, crossing her arms over her chest. "Before I tell you anything, I want assurances."

"What assurances?" Nick bit out.

"Immunity, for one."

"You haven't given us anything to grant you that," Nick snapped.

"Well, I still don't trust that—" Myia began.

"Myia," Adrian interrupted. She was trying her best, but her patience was also wearing thin. "Again, we're not interested in you or whatever your activities are. We're only interested in stopping dangerous people from finding Atlantis. The most we can promise for now is to not ask how you obtained any information you provide. If that's still not enough, we walk—but so does a potential reward for helping us."

Adrian didn't mention that she wasn't even certain she could get that reward. But now was the time to draw the line in the sand; Myia was clearly the type to take advantage of having even the slightest benefit in a given situation.

Myia's mouth tightened. Elias stepped forward

and murmured something in her ear. Her eyes closed, and she let out a sigh.

"Socrates' real name was Ben Grant. He's—he was—originally from Australia. We were . . . friends," she said, her voice catching slightly. "He found artifacts through . . . questionable means and sold them to the highest bidder. He knew what he did was dangerous, but he was always extremely careful. I don't know how this could have happened."

"The artifact that Socrates—Ben—showed Elias," Adrian said gently. "Do you know anything about it? How he obtained it?"

"He sent me a photo," Myia said, after hesitating for a beat. "He didn't tell me exactly where he found it, he just told me he only showed it to a curator friend of his to have it verified."

"Do you have the photo?" Nick asked.

"I want to know about this reward," Myia said.

"Show us what you have first," Adrian returned.

Myia glanced at Elias, who gave her an encouraging nod. She gestured for them to follow her, leading them to a study. She left them there, returning a few moments later with a laptop. She opened it, typing in a password before setting it down on the large desk to face them.

Adrian froze at the image that filled the laptop screen. It was the same inscription Elias had shown her, but there was *more* of it, the clay shards it was inscribed on partially pieced back together.

The markings were all Linear A, with the only familiar markings of the pre-Greek word for Atlantis.

"I need to show this to our team in DC," she said.

Myia tensed, but Adrian leveled her with a hard stare, her patience at an end. "Myia, we don't have a choice. This is the one piece of evidence outside of the Solon papyrus that could lead us to Atlantis. If you want that reward, we're going to need help. And I'm not asking your permission," she added firmly.

Myia glared, but seemed to realize that she had no choice in the matter, especially when Nick placed his tall frame protectively in front of the laptop. Adrian kept her gaze trained on Myia as she took out her phone and placed a call to the task force, putting it on speaker.

Vince was the one who answered. "If it isn't the intrepid duo," he said. "I assume you're only calling us because you need something? We are going to have to work on this relationship. There needs to be more back and forth."

Despite the tension of the moment, Adrian's lips quirked with amusement.

"We can work on it," she said. "But for now, we need help deciphering a three-thousand-year-old writing system."

CHAPTER 13

Athens, Greece
10:15 P.M.

Stephanos entered the dining room that overlooked one of the swimming pools on his property, greeting the three senior members of CHSR who were waiting for him there. As far as he was concerned, they were his true allies—and some of the wealthiest benefactors of the organization, whose resources were invaluable to his plans. They were Iris and Spiros Kalyvas, a married couple in their forties; Iris was an heiress to her father's banking fortune, and Viktor Drossos, an oil and gas tycoon Stephanos' age, who believed as fervently as he did in the ancient wisdom.

They knew what his plans were and stood with him.

He had asked them here to tell them in person about the recent setbacks he'd experienced in pursuit of Atlantis. He figured it was better to get in front of everything and reassure them that all was still going according to plan, despite his own frustration at the setbacks.

"In your message, you mentioned a setback," Iris said shortly, as soon as he greeted them. "What's happening? Are you making progress with the papyrus?"

Stephanos stiffened. He didn't like her demeaning tone. It reminded him of the way the other board members had spoken to him.

"My team is working on it as we speak, and they will have results shortly," Stephanos lied. "As for the inscription found on the shards, our contact in Heraklion refused to tell us where he found them, which would greatly help my experts with decipherment. Since he didn't cooperate, we unfortunately had to take care of him."

"You seem confident despite your lack of progress," Spiros said shortly. "When the papyrus was found, you told us it was only a matter of time before you'd locate Atlantis."

"It is only a matter of time," Stephanos said, struggling to keep his voice calm. He hated that they were challenging him. They were all supposed to be on the same side. "But with a find of this scale, there are bound to be initial setbacks."

"You haven't halted our other plans, have you? It seems you've lost focus ever since the papyrus was discovered," Iris said with a frown.

"My people are still working in the background," Stephanos said shortly. He took a breath for calm before continuing. "But don't you see? Atlantis is the key to all of this. If what we seek is there, it will speed up my—our—plans."

Yet they still looked uncertain. Anger rose in Stephanos' gut. They were lucky he had chosen to include them in his plans, and now they doubted him. Even his supposed allies were against him. He forced a smile. "I should let you get back to your homes. My driver will take you back, of course. I'll keep you updated with any progress."

They filed out, leaving him alone. He moved to the floor-to-ceiling windows, his eyes going to the night sky. Stephanos missed his father greatly at times like these; he was the only one who saw Stephanos' brilliance for what it was.

"They don't understand you, *agape mou*," a sultry voice murmured from behind him. "But I do."

Stephanos stiffened with irritation. "You're supposed to be searching for Elias Mandreou and those two American agents. What are you still doing here?"

"You want me to leave? You don't want to hear what information I have for you?"

He stilled, turning to face Irina. She looked quite pleased with herself, leaning against the doorframe with a smirk.

He studied her. Irina had been a mercenary assassin introduced to him by a weapons dealer. When he realized that she was as ruthless as he was, and fiercely loyal, he'd hired her on to his personal security detail, but she had become so much more. He didn't know much about her background, only that she had no family, and he got the sense that she'd been on her own for a long time, perhaps most of her life. She'd do whatever it took to survive.

He stalked toward her, wrapping his hand around her throat. Rather than looking fearful, there was arousal in Irina's eyes. She even leaned into his touch. *Crazy bitch.* But he had to admit, he found her lack of fear sexy. He'd always found Irina's fearlessness sexy, even when she was irritating him—like right now.

"Don't play games with me," he hissed.

"I'm not."

"Then what are you talking about?"

"First, I want your word that I'll get a cut of the treasure you find at Atlantis. And I want you to stop treating me like a needy girlfriend. We may have been lovers, but I'm one of your most loyal soldiers. Don't forget that," Iris said, her playfulness gone, her green eyes flashing fire.

Stephanos glared down at her, both furious and aroused. He didn't want to promise her anything, but if she knew something of value . . .

"As long as what you have to tell me helps lead to Atlantis," he snapped.

"It does. In a way."

"In a way? Irina—"

"Do you want my information or not?"

"Fine," he said through gritted teeth. "Now. What is it?"

She leaned in close, so that their lips were almost touching. "There is someone in the organization who is actively working against you, Stephanos. They don't want you to find Atlantis."

∽

12:03 A.M.

RESTLESS, Adrian paced the length of the living room, her mind racing.

She and Nick had connected with Layla, the linguist from the task force, showing her the inscriptions. After taking them in with awe, Layla had informed them that while she was familiar with Linear A, she still needed input from a linguist contact at the CIA, who knew even more about the writing system to help decipher any part of it.

"But it's still going to be a long shot," Layla warned. "Even with what we have from the papyrus, linguists still haven't been able to conclusively decrypt Linear A."

"We'll take whatever we can get," Adrian replied. She knew that even if Layla and her contact could only decrypt one or two words, that could point them in the right direction.

Elias and Myia hovered in the corner of the room; Myia looking morose and grief-stricken, Elias pale and shaken. She knew they were both still reeling over Socrates' murder.

Nick watched Adrian warily, his arms crossed over his chest. He had watched her restless pacing during many late nights working cases during their early days at the bureau. Still, he had reached out to take her hand, causing that familiar awareness at his touch to flare to life.

"You should try to get some rest, West," he urged.

"No way. You know me, Nick. I'm not going to sleep until I get answers."

He dropped his hand with a sigh, and she tried not to notice how much she missed his brief touch before she resumed pacing.

She was also worried about the person who'd killed Socrates. Had they somehow gotten their hands on the artifact? Were they already ahead of them and knew where the inscriptions pointed to?

A ping sounded on Myia's laptop, indicating an incoming call. Adrian and the others hurried over to it and answered. Layla's face appeared on the screen.

"Here's where we are," she said. "We were able to guess at two words from the inscription. We did a loose transliteration using the logograms, by comparing them to the Linear B writing system."

"Layman's terms for us non linguists?" Nick asked, raising his eyebrows.

"We derived phonetic values from the syllabic sounds of Linear B," Layla said. She shared her computer screen with them, zooming in on two of the inscriptions. "It's possible that this stands for *Di-kta*—and this one, *wa-na-ka*. We're going to see if we can guess at some other words, but I can't make any promises."

"This is great, Layla," Adrian said. "Thanks."

"'Dikta' and 'wanaka,'" Nick said, turning to face her with a frown after Layla had logged off. "Any idea what those words could mean?"

"'Dikta' is probably an alternate spelling that refers to a mountain range in eastern Crete—the Dikti Mountains," Elias said slowly.

"And 'wanaka' is the stem of the Greek word 'anax,' which means leader or king," Adrian added, thinking out loud. "Its origins are believed to be pre-Greek and later borrowed into the Greek language. Anax was used in the *Iliad* to refer to Agamemnon, a Mycenaean king. Anax is also sometimes used in modern Greek to refer to royalty."

"OK. So we have an ancient word for Atlantis, a word that could refer to the Dikti mountain range and the word for king," Nick said. "Anyone got any ideas?"

Myia shrugged while Elias looked deep in thought. Adrian drummed her fingers on the desk, turning to face Elias.

"What can you tell us about the Minoan civilization?" she asked.

"Well, it was an advanced civilization that thrived on Crete during the Bronze Age. Many historians consider it to be one of the first—if not the first—advanced civilizations in Europe. They had art, architecture, a writing system, and likely dominated trade in the Mediterranean. There is some debate about what brought about its fall, but the consensus is that it was a combination of factors —invasion by the Mycenaean Greeks and an eruption on the nearby island of Santorini, which destabilized the climate, affecting the island's natural resources," Elias said. "After its fall, it gradually fell out of memory until its rediscovery by Arthur Evans."

"Arthur Evans," Nick said, rolling his eyes. "I've heard of that guy."

Adrian gave Nick a rueful grin. Arthur Evans was a British archaeologist who discovered the palatial complex of Knossos, which he dubbed the Palace of Minos. This led to the rediscovery of the Minoan civilization, so named for the mythical King Minos from Greek mythology. Evans earned the scorn of many historians when he rebuilt walls, rooms, and columns of the complex during restoration, to the horror of archaeologists. Though modern historians now recognized and praised Evans for his discovery of a long-forgotten civilization, the controversy of his actions continued to linger long after his death.

Adrian's thoughts turned from Evans to the downfall of this great civilization. What was the link to Atlantis? The words king and Dikta added little to unraveling the mystery. They needed more.

"There is something else that Dikta could refer to," Elias said. "There's a theory that the Minoan name Dikta actually referred to ancient Zakros, and there are mentions in ancient writings that Dikta was a mountain *and* a place. The ancient Greek historian Diodorus mentions in his writings that the god Zeus founded a city near Dikti, the legendary place of his birth."

"Zakros?" Myia interjected. "As in the Minoan palace of Zakros?"

"That's the one," Elias said. He turned to Adrian and Nick. "Most people have heard of the palace of Knossos—that's the one that drives much of Crete's tourism. Zakros is another Minoan palace in eastern Crete. It's the latest to be discovered, the most isolated of the three Minoan-era palaces on Crete. But it was of great importance; it was roughly eight thousand square meters with one hundred and fifty rooms. Trade was its primary focus, and given its location in the east, its trade was focused on eastern routes."

Adrian looked at Nick, her heart picking up its pace. If Elias was right, they had somewhere concrete to look.

"Where were the excavated artifacts from Zakros taken?" she asked.

"To the Heraklion Archaeological Museum," Elias said. "And I just so happen to have a contact there who can help us."

CHAPTER 14

Athens, Greece
12:32 A.M.

Athena sat up in her hospital bed, rubbing the sleep from her eyes as her boss, Police Sergeant Yiannis Stergiou, and a tall, well-built, blond man she didn't recognize, entered her room. She'd been drifting off to sleep when a nurse had asked if she was willing to have visitors at such a late hour. Athena had agreed, assuming it was Stavros again. Surprise flitted through her at the sight of her boss and this other man.

"Sorry to visit you at such a late hour," Yiannis said. "How are you feeling?"

"Fine. Just tired and eager to get out of here," she said. "What's going on? Has there been a development on the case?"

Yiannis heaved a sigh, his brows knitting with worry. "No, unfortunately. This is Police Lieutenant Tobias Vasileiou," he said, gesturing to the other man, who offered her a stiff nod. "We're here about your partner. Stavros hasn't been seen since leaving your room earlier. He didn't show up to a meeting about the case at headquarters, which you know isn't like him. I called his wife; she hasn't seen him since he left to come visit you. And he's not answering his phone."

Panic flared in her chest as she thought of Stavros' caginess earlier. It had to be linked. She cursed herself for not pressing him on it. What if he was in danger? Caught up in something over his head—something related to this case?

She swallowed, her gaze shifting to the lieutenant. As worried as she was about Stavros, she was even more confused about why he was here. A missing investigator was well beneath his pay grade.

"I happened to be in your boss' office when the call came in about your missing partner," he said, as if reading her mind. "Given the importance of the case you're working on, I wanted to assist. Did Stavros mention anything in particular while he was here? Anything else besides the case?"

Unease prickled at her spine as she recalled Stavros' words to her earlier. Though he was her superior, there was something about Tobias that she didn't trust.

"No," she lied, holding his gaze. "We just talked about the case. He urged me to get some rest and then he left."

"Are you sure?" Tobias pressed. "Anything at all can help us with locating him."

"I wish I had more information," she said stiffly.

Frustration flitted across Tobias' face, but he gave her a tight smile.

"OK. Well, we'll leave you to your recuperation, and we'll, of course, keep you up to date with our search for your partner. Before we go, I did want to personally let you know that we're giving you extended time off in light of your injury."

"I'm fine," Athena said, shaking her head. "I don't even need to be in the hospital. I'm just here for observation. I'm perfectly capable of—"

"We can hardly have an investigator shot in the line of duty not take time off for much needed rest," Tobias said. He was still smiling, but his tone was pure steel. "I'm going to have to insist. We have all of your notes and a capable team working with other agencies on this case."

Anger and frustration surged through her. Yiannis looked apologetic, but subtly shook his head. She had to take several deep breaths to calm herself, offering Tobias a nod as she prepared herself to tell another lie.

"OK," she said finally. "I understand."

"Good. And again, please contact us immediately if you hear from Stavros."

They headed out, with Yiannis hesitating for a moment before following Tobias out of the room.

Athena remained still for a good twenty minutes, her heart racing, before sliding out of the bed. Now that she knew Stavros was missing, she was wide awake, and she wasn't going to waste another second lying in this damn hospital bed. Something else was going on here, and with the lieutenant's visit, she had a dark feeling that her own department was involved. Now she was even more determined to find out exactly what it was.

But first, she had to find her partner.

Heraklion, Crete
1:17 A.M.

ADRIAN PULLED their rental car to a stop several blocks away from the Heraklion Museum, where they were meeting Elias' contact, Kostas, a curator there.

Elias had left the room to place a call to Kostas, convincing him to show them the Zakros collection at the museum at this late hour. He'd fed Kostas a story about a last-minute lecture he was giving at the University of Crete and desperately needed to fact-check an item from the collection—in person.

"Fortunately for us," Elias said with a wry smile, "I'm known for my procrastination and needing things last minute."

Still, Adrian noticed that Elias seemed incredibly nervous since placing the call, so much so that Myia had asked him several times if he was all right during their drive to the museum.

"I'm fine," Elias replied, giving her a forced smile. "I'm just hoping we're on the right track."

A black SUV was already parked in front of them, and as soon as they got out, a stout, bald man, who Adrian assumed was Kostas, approached them.

Adrian stiffened as he drew closer. Something seemed . . . off about him. His smile was tight, his body rigid with tension, even as he gave Elias a handshake and Elias introduced them all. Her eyes strayed to Elias, whose body language also radiated discomfort. She'd bought his reasoning for being nervous earlier, but seeing similar behavior from Kostas, her hackles were raised. What was going on?

"Because of security protocols, I'm going to need you to remove your service weapons before we go inside," Kostas said, not meeting their eyes.

"No," Nick said immediately, looking as suspicious as she felt. "We're federal agents, and we—"

The door to the SUV opened, and an imposingly large, dark-haired man, with a jagged scar on his cheek, stepped out, leveling a weapon at their chests.

"I'd advise you to listen to the man," he said calmly.

CHAPTER 15

Three other men climbed out of the SUV, aiming pistols at them.

Panic flooded Adrian, her body stiffening. Her instincts had certainly been right about something being off.

But who were these men? Had Kostas tipped them off?

Her answer came instantaneously. The man, still staring at Adrian, Nick, and Myia, addressed Elias.

"Thank you for your assistance, Elias," he said.

Adrian's gaze flew to Elias. He averted his eyes. His face had gone pale, his expression infused with shame.

She silently cursed herself. How could she have missed this? She'd suspected Elias was still holding something back from them, but she hadn't even considered that he was working for the other side. But now that she thought about it, his summoning her to his hospital room, his continued caginess, and odd nervousness on the way to the museum now made sense.

Adrian made herself suppress her tangle of emotions. She didn't have time to wallow in her sense of shame, embarrassment, and betrayal. The man was still staring at her coldly, his pistol aimed at her chest.

She shot a quick glance at Nick. They could risk trying to fight their way out of this, but they were outnumbered, and she didn't know if these men had even more backup. It was too risky.

Adrian swallowed hard, taking out her service weapon and tossing it to the ground. Nick and Myia followed suit.

"Good choice," the man said, giving her a nod. "Now walk. Slowly. We won't hesitate to shoot you. And when we shoot, we shoot to kill."

As they made their way toward the museum, the men surrounding them in a tight formation, Adrian tried to calm her racing thoughts. *Think.* The security cameras at the museum—and security itself—had likely been taken care of, so there would be no help on that front.

Nick, who was walking close to her side, looked as intensely deep in thought as she was, no doubt also considering how to get out of this. Myia, walking on her other side, was practically shaking with fury, glaring at the back of Elias' head. As someone who knew Elias, Adrian could only imagine the depth of betrayal she must have felt. A renewed sense of anger filled her as her own gaze fell on Elias, who walked stiffly alongside the man, whom one of the other men addressed as Michalis. She urged herself to quell it. She just needed to focus on getting them out of this, and she needed calm to do so.

They reached the side entrance to the museum, where a visibly shaken Kostas used his key card for entry. She studied Kostas. Given his demeanor, he was not a willing participant in this. Michalis had likely threatened him. Could he be a key to their escape?

Kostas met her gaze, but quickly looked away. She had the distinct feeling he would only care about keeping himself safe, and he seemed terrified of Michalis. She needed to think of another way.

Kostas led them inside the museum. In contrast to the ancient artifacts it housed, the Heraklion Museum was of modern architectural design with well-lit floors, featuring spacious exhibition spaces, which covered thousands of years of Cretan history, and the world's largest collection of Minoan artifacts, from sculptures to pottery to ancient seals and jewelry. Adrian had never been here before, but this wasn't the time to admire the treasures that surrounded them as they made their way down a long corridor and past the exhibition rooms that featured various Minoan artifacts. She subtly scanned for exits, but could barely see beyond the men who encircled them.

Kostas led them to the exhibition space that

was dedicated solely to findings from Zakros. Only then did the men step back, giving them room to move, but watching each of them like hawks.

Adrian stepped forward, trying to look as if she were concentrating on taking in the artifacts in their display cases, from pottery to vases to rhytons, which were drinking containers for libation rituals. But all she could think about was how to get out of their predicament.

"We're hoping to find something that pointed to Atlantis among these artifacts, given that the inscription on the shards could point to Zakros palace," Elias told Michalis, stepping forward, his eyes scanning over the artifacts.

"Like what?" Michalis asked impatiently.

"We don't know," Elias said, turning to look at Adrian and Nick, as if for justification. Nick glared while Adrian kept her expression neutral. "A symbol, an inscription..."

Michalis turned his gaze to her, and Adrian forced herself to step forward, concentrating on the artifacts before her. If she could give Michalis something—even something false—there was a way out of this.

Her gaze landed on rhytons with detailed engravings that depicted open-air religious sanctuaries, with Minoan religious symbols, such as the horns of consecration hovering above them. She took in the other artifacts, noticing a common motif of marine or floral designs along with religious symbology, but there was no smoking gun, nothing that linked to what they'd found so far that could point toward Atlantis.

"I'm not seeing anything," Elias said with a frustrated sigh. He turned to Kostas. "Are there any more artifacts in storage from the site?"

"N—not currently," Kostas stammered, sliding a fearful look at Michalis.

Elias turned to Michalis. "I don't think we're going to find what we're looking for here."

"Why not?" Michalis demanded, his tone sharp and dangerous. "On the phone, you told me—"

"I told you I *thought* there may be something here. But it's looking like I was wrong," Elias said. "The inscription on the shards—I still think it's significant that it could mention Zakros. There may be something at the archaeological site itself that we're missing here. It's a three-hour drive east from here, but we can get there faster, given the time of night," Elias added.

Michalis narrowed his eyes, taking a menacing step forward. "If you're lying to me, you know what's at stake."

Adrian kept her expression neutral, though surprise flared within her. Elias hadn't mentioned going directly to the palace before, insisting that the artifacts excavated from the site were the ones that contained answers. Was he stalling? Trying to help them get out of this? Or was that just wishful thinking on her part?

Elias gave Michalis a shaky nod. Adrian's profiler brain was trying to keep up. She didn't know if she could trust Elias or not, and clearly, neither did their captor. She did know that going to another location, far from this one, was their best chance at attempting an escape.

Michalis turned to Adrian, Nick, and Myia, giving them a deadly look. "We'll head to Zakros in separate cars. If any of you try anything, my men will shoot all of you, no questions asked. Am I understood?"

He waited for their nods before turning to his men, barking orders at them in Greek. Adrian and Nick made the briefest of eye contact, his expression stoic, but she knew that Nick was on the same page. This was their opportunity to escape.

She could only pray they survived the attempt.

2:02 A.M.

NICK GRITTED his teeth as one of the men shoved him into the back of a waiting car. They'd put Adrian and Elias into the SUV, and himself and Myia into another dark car parked in front of it. Nick hated being separated from Adrian, though he knew his partner was more than capable of handling herself.

He was soon wedged in between Myia and the same man who had shoved him in, and one of the other men took the driver's seat. Myia stared straight ahead, her teeth clenched. She didn't look even remotely frightened, just pissed off. He wanted to get her attention, but didn't know how to without alerting the two men. For his plan to work, they both needed to be in on it. Since he didn't have time to communicate with her, he needed to just act. Time was of the essence. He just hoped she was good at improvising.

Nick did a mental size-up of the two men. The man in the back, with him and Myia, was large and broad, but meaty—he wouldn't be as quick as Nick. The driver was only slightly smaller, but that didn't mean he wasn't strong. Nick would have to act very, very fast . . . or he was at risk of killing all of them.

Nick remained stock still, his gaze trained straight ahead as the driver started the car and pulled onto the road. He purposefully kept his breathing very steady, something he'd learned to do during his training at the academy, forcing the adrenaline down.

He'd need all of it very soon.

Their car made its way onto the highway leading out of Heraklion. Nick waited, his heart thudding steadily, until their car made a turn onto an isolated stretch of road. Up ahead, there was a sharp curve, and he knew that this was his opportunity.

He subtly nudged Myia's leg with his. Myia didn't react, keeping her gaze trained straight ahead, but he knew she'd felt it. She was either ignoring him or had a great poker face. He prayed it was the latter.

Nick counted down to three. As the car approached the curve in the road—

He sprang into action, lunging forward.

CHAPTER 16

Adrian knew she would strike; she just didn't know when.

As soon as she saw the car with Nick and Myia in it swerve abruptly to the right, the decision was made for her.

Adrian was seated in the back of the SUV, wedged between Elias and one of Michalis' men to her right, with Michalis in the front passenger seat next to the driver. She didn't trust Elias, so she moved without alerting him, taking advantage of the element of surprise to jab the guard next to her in the face with her elbow. Startled and letting out a howl of pain, he dropped his weapon. Before he could retaliate, Adrian jabbed him a second time in the eye.

In the front seat, Michalis turned to face her with a snarl, raising his weapon. Moving as fast as she could, Adrian hurled her body forward, knocking the weapon from his hand and lurching toward the steering wheel, jerking it violently to the right, even as the driver tried to fight her off—

The driver pressed on the brakes as the car swerved, but he'd already lost control. Adrian moved back and curled up into a ball on the floor behind the passenger seat, getting herself into a brace position as the SUV careened to the side of the road, slamming into the back of the other car with a sickening crush.

The impact hurled Adrian against the side door, and pain radiated down her spine.

Grimacing, she forced herself to straighten. The guard in the back seat was slumped over against the side of the door, unconscious. Elias looked dazed; he had a nasty cut on the side of his temple but otherwise seemed uninjured.

The driver was hunched over the steering wheel, completely still. Michalis had also lurched forward, but she could hear his ragged breaths.

Ignoring the pain that spiraled down her back, Adrian reached for the guard's weapon on the floor and pushed past Elias, opening the door. As soon as she was out, she whirled to face Elias, leveling the weapon at his chest. Elias' face went ashen, and he held up his hands.

"Please—I—" he began.

"Get out and on your knees. Hands where I can see them," she barked.

Elias complied, and she stalked over to the passenger's side door. Michalis had come to and was struggling to open his door.

Adrian swung it open. Michalis lunged for her, but she brought down the butt of her gun onto his temple with as much force as she could muster. Michalis slumped over, unconscious.

She stumbled back, breathing through her pain. She turned to see Nick and Myia climbing out of the car in front of them, both handling the unconscious bodies of the driver and the guard. Adrian stalked back over to Elias, who was still obediently on his knees, trembling, hands raised.

"Please—I had no choice. They threatened to kill my fiancée," he said, his voice breaking.

Adrian studied him closely. For the first time, she saw genuine emotion in his eyes. He was being truthful with her. She lowered her weapon, taking several calming breaths. As angry as she was with him, and as much as she still didn't trust him, she needed whatever information he had.

Myia approached, marching toward Elias, aiming her gun at him, eyes wild with rage.

"Myia!" Adrian shouted.

Myia ignored her. Just as her finger started to pull the trigger, Nick tackled her to the ground from behind, disarming her. Myia struggled against him, her dark eyes spitting fire at Elias.

"Are you working for them?!" she shouted. "Do you know what they've done to me? To my family?! I trusted you!"

Adrian froze, looking back and forth between Elias' confused, stricken face and Myia's furious one. What was Myia talking about? Adrian had a million more questions, but now was not the time.

"We don't have time for this," she hissed. "We need to contact the local police and get these men into custody." She gave Elias a hard look. "And then we need to get some answers."

CHAPTER 17

Hersonissos, Crete
4:08 A.M.

"Talk," Adrian said sharply to Elias.

She, Nick, and Elias were in an empty waiting room in the small police station in Hersonissos, the nearest town to where they'd crashed. Hersonissos was popular with tourists who wanted to escape the city of Heraklion and enjoy the beaches of the Mediterranean.

She could tell the local police were overwhelmed when they'd arrived at the scene. After Adrian and Nick had shown the police their credentials, they'd taken their statements and brought Michalis, along with one of his men into custody; they'd taken the other two men to a local hospital to treat their injuries. The police had sent an officer to both the museum and Kostas' address, but the curator had already fled.

The paramedics who'd arrived at the scene had looked them over, taking care of Elias' cut and giving Adrian painkillers for her sore back, telling them they were both lucky their injuries weren't more serious.

Myia, distrustful and wary of police officers, was waiting for them outside the station in their rental that the police had retrieved for them. Adrian had questions for Myia as well, in light of what she'd revealed when screaming at Elias, but she'd opted to wait until after she'd spoken to Elias. She wanted to give Myia more time to calm down.

Nick had contacted the police in Athens to update them; they were arranging the transport of Michalis and his men to the police headquarters there for questioning. Michalis and his colleague were in a holding cell here until they could be transported to Athens. Adrian had tried to question Michalis and his underling, but they were both brick walls, looking right through her and refusing to answer any question she asked. Frustrated, she and Nick had turned their focus to Elias.

She'd decided against telling the police that Elias was working with Michalis and his men—at least for now. There were answers she wanted to get for herself first.

Elias was sitting quietly, still looking shaken, his hands resting on his knees. He didn't answer Adrian's prodding right away. Nick stepped forward, glowering at him.

"*Talk*," Nick repeated. "Right now."

Nick had been opposed to not telling the police about Elias. While he wasn't as furious as Myia, he was still on edge, and had only reluctantly agreed with Adrian's plan as long as they got answers from Elias.

"Michalis approached me a month before the papyrus was stolen. I didn't know he was planning to steal it. I swear," he added quickly. "He told me I was going to help him with something, or he was going to kill—" He took a deep, shuddering breath. "My fiancée. I didn't believe him at first. So . . . he had someone beat her up to prove how serious he was. Landed her in the hospital. He then told me he'd kill not only my fiancée, but my other family members as well."

"What exactly did he want from you?" Adrian asked.

"He knew of my expertise in ancient Mediterranean civilizations and wanted me to supply any information I had in regards to the papyrus and where it could lead to. After they stole the papyrus, I was told to work with the police and supply him with any information the investigation unearthed—specifically from other experts they brought in to assist. When Michalis—or rather, the people he was working for—learned that you were on the case, Adrian, I was told to ask you to come to the hospital and offer my services." He looked down, shame flickering across his face. "I didn't want to do any of it, especially after they stole the papyrus . . . but I couldn't risk my family's lives."

"How were you injured in the explosion if you were working with them?" Nick asked.

"Wrong place, wrong time," Elias said with a regretful shake of his head. "And again, I didn't know they were planning to steal the papyrus. I happened to be near the entrance when the explosions went off. I didn't know that was going to happen. I'm expendable—they may have others working for them. My injury did seem to work in their favor, though. It was shortly after that I was told to contact you when I was in the hospital."

"Them? Myia also mentioned a 'them.' Is this some type of group?" Adrian asked sharply.

"I don't know what Myia's talking about," Elias said, looking genuinely confused. "I was only ever contacted by Michalis . . . but he always seemed like a foot soldier, like he was taking orders from someone else."

Adrian considered this. They needed to find out who Michalis was working for.

"Those two men who came after you in the hospital—" Nick began.

"No idea who they were," Elias said, his face going pale. "At first, I assumed they were after me because they thought I'd told you the truth about working for Michalis. But when I contacted Michalis in Heraklion, he insisted he'd not been the one to send those men after me—I was safe as long as I kept playing along."

"And you believed him?" Nick challenged.

"For now. They still need—or needed me. If

they wanted me dead, I wouldn't be here," Elias said shakily.

Adrian studied him; he looked terrified at the memory and seemed to be telling the truth. It made no sense that Michalis, or his employer, would send someone after Elias if he was working for them, which added another layer to the mystery.

"What about Socrates' death?" Nick challenged. "Did you—"

"God, no," Elias whispered. "I was as shocked as you were. And I was telling the truth about not showing him the papyrus. He must have found out about it some other way. I came close to confessing then, but I was terrified. It showed these people were willing to kill. I couldn't risk my family."

"And your suggestion of going to Zakros?" Adrian asked. "Was that genuine or—"

"I wanted to give us a chance to escape. There's nothing, as far as I know, that would have helped us at Zakros. Anything of note, writings or artifacts, would have been excavated and sent to the museum," Elias replied.

Nick still glared at Elias, his arms crossed over his chest. Adrian recalled her time on the Cleopatra case, when her friend Sebastian Rossi was kidnapped and forced to work with his abductors. If Elias was telling the truth—and a simple fact check could prove that—he was no different.

"OK. We won't turn you in," she said finally.

Nick stiffened. "Adrian—"

"On the strict condition that you work for us

now. We can have our task force get your family to safety." Adrian leaned forward, fixing him with a hard stare. "But if you so much as breathe wrong, I will personally make sure you are brought up on so many charges you spend the rest of your life—and any life beyond that—in prison."

Elias nodded, giving her a look of gratitude. "Thank you. I'll—"

"*Adrian,*" Nick repeated, his voice tight. "Can I talk to you?"

He led her out of the room, shutting the door behind him. Adrian held up her hands, giving him an imploring look.

"I know you don't like this, but I believe he's telling the truth. We can still use his expertise. If we turn him in, we risk—" she began.

"Agent West. Agent Harper."

Adrian and Nick turned. One of the police officers, Officer Lucas Dimou, who'd brought Michalis and the other man into custody, stood behind them, his expression grim.

"What is it?" Nick demanded.

"Your prisoners," he said. "They—they're gone."

CHAPTER 18

Hersonissos, Crete
6:38 A.M.

Michalis had vanished into thin air.

The police performed a sweep of the jail and the surrounding area, but they found no trace of him.

Adrian was suspicious; the only way he could have gotten out was with help. Conveniently, the lone security camera at the station was down, so she had no proof that one of the officers had helped him escape. Whoever was helping Michalis had moved quickly.

Adrian turned away from the window of the hotel room they'd booked close to the police station. Fatigue was weighing down on her; none of them had slept a wink. She and Nick had alerted the authorities in both Athens and DC, and an APB had been sent out for Michalis. They also gave

Vince and Jonathan, from the task force, the phone number Michalis had used to contact Elias. They'd decided to not mention their suspicions of the local police's involvement to the authorities in Athens. She didn't want to believe that the police in Athens were also connected to this, but after the revelation of Elias' betrayal, they couldn't be too careful.

"This is why I don't trust the authorities," Myia said. She was straddling a chair, glaring at Elias, who was seated across the room from her at the desk. They'd had to keep Myia and Elias physically apart; Myia was still furious and distrustful of him, even after Adrian explained her reasoning for keeping him with them. "There's no way that bastard could have escaped without the police's help."

Adrian turned to face Myia. A part of her had feared that Myia would flee once the police were involved; she'd been relieved to find her waiting for them when they'd left the police station. Adrian suspected that this was now more about reward money for Myia. After Socrates' murder and now Elias' involvement, it was personal.

"Who were you referring to when you confronted Elias about working for 'them'? And what did they do to your family?" Adrian asked.

Myia lowered her gaze, and the silence stretched for so long that Adrian didn't think she'd answer. Finally, Myia spoke, getting up from the chair.

"My mother . . . she was a part of an organization when I was a kid. She never told me its name, but it sounded very much like a secret society. She told me it was very old, going back to the time of the ancient Greeks. The purpose of it was to find a lost civilization and ancient knowledge that the civilization held, but she never told me exactly what civilization it was. By the time I was a teenager, she told me it had broken off from its initial beliefs, its teachings. There were some men and women at the top who wanted to find this lost civilization to bring about the end of ours. Now I know that she was referring to Atlantis. When members, including my mother, protested this new purpose, they started to disappear. She grew paranoid and constantly thought she was being followed. We began to move—frequently." Myia closed her eyes briefly, lost in the past. "When I went away to college, things seemed to have calmed, and I thought the threat was gone. But when I came back for a visit one day, I found my mother dead in her bedroom. Pills. The police told me it was a suicide. For all my mother's paranoia, she was never depressed—not even remotely suicidal. I knew it was them. This organization," she spat, fury flaring in her eyes.

A surge of empathy filled Adrian. She could recall her own feeling of helplessness after her father disappeared years ago . . . her desperation to find out what happened to him. That feeling never went away.

"The police thought I was crazy when I told

them about this organization, especially because I couldn't give them any specific details about exactly what it was. I didn't even have a name. That's when I lost my trust in . . . everything. I dropped out of university, lived off the grid, did what I could to make money. I tried to find out more about what my mother was involved in, but these people, this organization, they're like ghosts. What happened to my mother has always been in the back of my mind. It wasn't until I saw him—Michalis—that it all came back to me. He was one of the men my mother thought was following her. I saw him once. I'll never forget that scar."

Adrian let Myia's words settle in, meeting Nick's gaze. Despite her fatigue, a renewed energy coursed through her. This organization sounded exactly like it could be behind all this. She recalled her initial profile of the thieves, how they were likely well-connected and well-funded.

"You mentioned the people at the top wanted to find this lost civilization to bring about the end of ours," Adrian said. "Did your mother ever mention how they planned to do this?"

"I remember her using the term 'ancient wisdom' when she referred to this organization. It was something that it sought from this lost civilization, Atlantis. Honestly, it seemed like some kind of code word for something else."

Ancient wisdom. What could be buried with Atlantis? What ancient wisdom could destroy current civilization?

An icy chill coursed through her at the realization of what it could be. She met Nick's eyes, and he looked just as uneasy. She knew what they were both thinking of . . . their recent investigation in the UK that had led them deep into the mountains of Russia.

"A weapon," Nick said, speaking her thoughts out loud. "Ancient wisdom could be a code word for a weapon."

"A weapon?" Myia asked, baffled. "What kind of weapon could be buried with Atlantis that could destroy civilization?"

Adrian turned to Elias. "How does the story of Atlantis end?"

"The gods sent calamities to Atlantis that caused it to sink beneath the sea. Earthquakes, floods, fires," he replied.

"Of those, the closest thing to a weapon I can think of is fire. What ancient weapon—" Adrian began.

"Oh my God," Elias interrupted, his face going ashen. "Greek fire. It was an incendiary weapon used in ancient times. Despite its name, it was used long before the ancient Greeks. It was fire that could burn even on the surface of water, incredibly effective in naval battles. We mostly know of it because of the Byzantine army, who used it to great effect, but they carefully guarded how it was made. There are theories, but even to this day, no one knows."

They all sat in silence for a moment, reeling.

Adrian told herself this was still just speculation, but given what Myia had just told them about this organization, it all made sense.

"Elias, do you know anything about this organization?"

"This is the first I'm hearing of it," Elias said. Adrian recalled how confused he'd looked back at the crash site when Myia had screamed at him. "And if I'd had any notion that Michalis worked for an organization looking for a weapon like this . . . "

"Why should we believe you?" Myia snapped.

"I told you—I had no choice," Elias responded tightly. "They were going to—"

"Save your lies." Myia clenched her fists at her sides. "Do you know who killed Socrates? Did you help—"

"No!" Elias cried, his expression going from contrite to enraged. "I was horrified at what happened to him, but it made me even more fearful of these people."

"You're a traitor, and I don't believe anything that you—"

"It's easy for you to—"

"Enough," Adrian interrupted. "Michalis is gone, but we know what he and this organization are possibly looking for. We just have to get there before they do."

Adrian swallowed, quelling her panic at the thought of this group getting their hands on an ancient weapon lying dormant within the ruins of Atlantis. She leaned forward, mulling over what they had so far. Solon's papyrus and the shard inscriptions. Perhaps they had made the wrong assumptions about the inscriptions. She recalled the two translated words, 'Dikta' and 'king'.

"The shards with the inscription. What do you think the shards belonged to? Is it possible it was a rhyton?" she asked, thinking of the rhytons she'd seen at the Heraklion Museum. "Or some other type of vessel used for religious rituals?"

"Like a libation vessel? That's possible," Elias replied, turning his heated gaze away from Myia.

"What was commonly written on artifacts found during this time period?" she pressed.

"Mostly administrative things—accounting, record keeping. Boring stuff. You probably know more than I do that writing was invented out of necessity. Everything else came later."

"So if there's an inscription on a libation vessel, it had to be important. Could it have been . . . a prayer?"

"That seems likely," Elias replied.

"And where would such an item typically be found?" Nick asked.

"Temples. Peak or cave sanctuaries," Elias said. At their questioning looks, he continued, "Peak and cave sanctuaries were spaces used for burial or religious rites found all throughout Minoan Crete. Peak sanctuaries were located on mountain peaks, in the open air, often visible from other peak sanctuaries. If the shards with the inscriptions had indeed belonged to a libation vessel, it would make sense that they were found at one such peak sanctuary.

"That word—Dikta," Nick said, looking at Adrian. "If not Zakros, it could be the old Occam's razor effect and just literally means the Dikti mountain rage."

"That would make sense," Myia said. "There are parts of that mountain range that are remote, and many unauthorized digs take place there. Socrates often went there," she added, her face shadowing with grief. Myia closed her eyes briefly, shaking her head as if clearing it before taking out her phone and pulling up a map. She held it up so they could all see, zooming in on a remote area of the mountain range.

"This is where he usually went," she said. "There's a village about twenty-five kilometers away, but other than that, it's far from all the popular hiking trails."

"With all those mountain peaks, this would have been a prime area for peak sanctuaries," Elias murmured, taking in the map.

"What are we waiting for?" Nick asked, turning to face them. "Time to brush off those hiking boots and climb ourselves a mountain."

CHAPTER 19

Athens, Greece
7:02 A.M.

"Michalis has been taken care of, as well as the men who were with him. We confirmed that they didn't learn anything beforehand, of course," Tobias Vasileiou said on the other end of the line.

Stephanos pressed his phone to his ear as he paced the length of his meditation room, where he'd gone to calm himself when he'd learned of this most recent setback in Heraklion. Yet the surroundings of the peaceful space hadn't calmed him. He was still shaking with fury.

Michalis had called Stephanos the previous evening, informing him that Elias had reached out with information he'd learned alongside the two American agents. Stephanos had been on the verge of taking his private plane to Heraklion when he learned Michalis had foolishly allowed himself to be taken into custody after the Americans had run their cars off the road. Michalis had been in his life for a long time. He'd sent him to Heraklion because he trusted him the most, which made his failure all the more disappointing. Yet he felt no remorse for his fate. Michalis knew what the cost of failure was.

A dark thought occurred to him. Ever since Irina told him someone was working against him, he'd been paranoid about all of his supposed allies in CHSR. Had Michalis' failure somehow been purposeful?

"I overheard parts of a late night meeting when I went to the CHSR offices to retrieve some files. The voices, which I didn't recognize, had discussed how your ideas were dangerous and you couldn't be trusted. They said you needed to be stopped. I had to leave before I was noticed, but I waited in the shadows outside. I saw Zacharias, Dmitris' son, and two other men I didn't recognize leave the building," Irina had told him.

He'd not wanted to believe Irina, but it all made sense. There was the board members' barely contained hostility toward him, going against him at every turn. There was the mystery of those two men who'd gone after his contact Elias in the hospital, whom he still didn't know the identity of. When Irina told him she'd seen Zacharias, it really fell into place. Dmitris and Zacharias had seemed to especially dislike him, which was odd, given how close Dmitris had been to his father.

Yet he wasn't able to make a move until he had definitive proof that Dmitris and Zacharias were working against him. If he eliminated them outright, there would be hell to pay with the other board members, including his allies, and he would risk exposing his plans. Instead, he was having Irina work in the background to find him the proof he needed, and to impede any efforts to slow him down.

His thoughts turned to the situation in Crete. If there was anything positive in this latest development, it was the power of CHSR's reach. One of the police officers at the station in Hersonissos belonged to the organization. He was the one who'd gotten Michalis out of custody, contacted the local mercenaries whom CHSR employed, handing Michalis and his men over to them. He had then contacted his main police contact in Athens, the lieutenant who also worked for CHSR: Tobias Vasileiou.

"And Elias?" Stephanos asked, though he already knew the answer. "The Americans? Where are they now?"

He could practically taste Tobias' discomfort on the other end of the line. "They left the station. We only have one officer working for us there, and that was pure luck. He was barely able to get Michalis out of custody. Had we detained the Americans, it would have raised an alarm. They've already contacted the authorities in Athens."

Though Stephanos knew Tobias was right, he

still let out a frustrated curse. He'd thought having Elias on their side would be a useful tool; now that had backfired. He knew the coward was now working with the Americans.

Expelling a breath, he abruptly ended his call with Tobias, placing another call to Irina. She answered on the first ring.

"I trust you heard about the debacle in Heraklion," he snapped.

"I did. I'm sorry for Michalis' failure, *agape mou*. And I'm still looking into Zacharias and his father. I—"

"This is about something else," he interrupted. "Elias and the Americans are looking into one of the Minoan palaces on Crete. I need our associates to send me everything they have on all the palaces from the Minoan era there. We need to look for anything we may have missed. And I want something concrete on Zacharias and his father soon, or I'm not certain I will even be able to trust you."

Stephanos hung up before Irina could respond, taking several deep, calming breaths, something he usually did at the start of his meditative practices.

He quelled his frustration, reminding himself what he was doing this for, what this would all lead to. He just needed patience. *The ancient wisdom*. Destruction leading to creation.

The founders of *Archaia Sofia* had agreed with the meaning behind Plato's work describing Atlantis, a society that deserved to fall because of hubris and greed. The founders believed the only way to fix a corrupt society was to destroy it and rebuild from its ashes. But that was when their world was mere city states, not the vast interconnection of societies it was today.

The world today was riddled with violence, greed, and corruption to its core, from the West with its capitalist oppression to the East with its tyrannical regimes. He could remember clearly when his father told him of his plans, just after his sixteenth birthday.

"The time has come for another collapse," his father told him, referring to the Bronze Age collapse during which multiple ancient societies had fallen around 1200 BCE. "Yes, it was a difficult time, and many died, but look what came from its ashes after the dark age that followed—the Greek city states, the Roman Empire, the birth of western civilization. A world reborn. Only this time we will make it even better with what we know now."

"How will we do it?" the young, naïve version of himself asked.

"I've already put the wheels in motion, son," his father replied with a smile.

It wasn't until years later that he learned the full extent of what his father had started, and what Stephanos had continued. Stephanos had inherited his father's wealth, which came from a mining and commodities company that he'd sold for millions and had put that wealth to use to further his father's plans. He had scientists from CHSR working in different sectors—researching how to weaponize viruses, and how to recreate the ancient weapon he believed was buried with Atlantis. He even had spies investigating the various ports, researching how to disrupt the supply chain to accelerate the devastation from upcoming wars or pandemics. With tensions between the world's nuclear powers constantly on the brink, it would only take a small push to inflame them to full nuclear war.

"The other leaders don't have the bravery that needs to do what needs to be done. They don't realize that the ancient wisdom that lies with Atlantis is its very destruction," his father once told him.

His father even had an extensive bunker tucked away in Switzerland for himself and a select group to flee to when the end came. With their resources, they would be ready to emerge and rebuild the destroyed world from its ashes.

But his father had died before his plans could come to fruition. Stephanos had held his hand at his bedside and whispered his promise that he would fulfill his dream, that he would do what was necessary. His father had given him a rare smile before drawing his last breath, seeming to take comfort in Stephanos' words.

The worldwide pandemic a few years back had given him hope he could easily bring the end about. It showed how precarious the modern, interconnected world was. Had the virus been more potent, paired with war or famine, it could have all ended then. If anything, the pandemic had shown how precariously close to the edge of collapse the world teetered, just as those advanced civilizations had centuries ago. But wasn't that the hubris of modern humanity? *There is nothing that can bring us down.* What fools.

When he'd learned of Solon's papyrus, something that could lead him directly to Atlantis and to the ancient weapon buried with it, he'd put all his time and resources into searching for it. The founders had written of a map that would lead directly to Atlantis, hidden on a papyrus by a great man. He'd hoped that the papyrus belonged to Solon, which is why he'd taken it on behalf of CHSR. Yet his team of paleographists had found nothing. There was no hint of a map on its fragments. The shard inscription had also given him nothing thus far. His experts were still attempting to decipher what they could from the fragments.

Stephanos expelled a breath, leaving his meditation room. He was going to keep his promise to his father. It was time to do what he'd done when he'd taken the papyrus himself. He was going to get more directly involved. He'd go to Crete himself. Given that Elias and those Americans had found something there, it looked as if that was where the answers were—answers he desperately needed to find Atlantis.

CHAPTER 20

Dikti Mountain Range
Katharon, Crete
9:12 A.M.

Myia maneuvered their rental truck down the road that wound through the Dikti mountain range as Adrian took in the vast landscape of rolling green plateaus that dotted the landscape beneath the mountains.

They'd only slept for a couple of hours before leaving their hotel to head to the mountains; Myia told them the ascent would take at least six hours, and it was best if they descended before nightfall. They'd traded in their rental car for a truck, taking side roads and using a fake ID Myia had in her possession in case they were being tracked. They had stopped at a sporting goods store in a town on their way east to pick up some mountain gear, with Myia paying in cash. Now that they believed the police were involved, out of an abundance of caution, they hadn't yet looped in the team in DC. For now, they were completely on their own. Adrian could only hope they were on the right track and that this remote site provided some answers.

Myia turned off the road, driving the truck forward until it was out of sight from the main road. They collected their backpacks and left the truck, trailing Myia toward the base of the mountain, which loomed before them like a colossus. Myia had assured them it was an easy climb that she'd made twice before with Socrates; it was a gradually ascending hike with only light rock climbing and no need for ropes, though she had bought a set just in case.

Still, the ascent from the ground looked daunting. Adrian kept in shape by jogging most mornings, but she hadn't climbed since her training days during the academy. Her back still had some minor soreness from the accident, though painkillers had helped tremendously. Nick was more than fit enough to handle the climb; she took in his tall, muscular form, unable to stop her gaze from lingering on him.

She caught Myia studying her as she took in Nick's form and quickly looked away. At her side, Elias was looking up at the mountain peaks, clear intimidation written across his face.

"Hey, the ancient Greeks did it," Nick said, as

if reading their minds. "They were certainly less healthy than we are."

"The people who made such treks would have been conditioned for such climbs," Elias said with a slight frown. Adrian's lips twitched with amusement. Even in his precarious position with them, he couldn't help himself. It was the plight of the historian to always be a historian, no matter the circumstances.

"Let's just hope there're some answers up there," Adrian said, thinking of what was at stake.

She ventured forward, trailing Myia up the base of the mountain, nervous anticipation coursing through her veins.

~

Athens, Greece
10:48 A.M.

"I CAN'T BELIEVE THIS," Helena Vlachis said, blinking away her tears. "It's like a nightmare."

Athena leaned forward and gripped Helena's hand. She was trying her damndest not to show it, but she was just as worried as Stavros' wife.

Last night, after leaving the hospital, she'd called Stavros' number at least a dozen times to no answer. She'd even gone to several of his favorite hangouts around Athens, though she knew he wouldn't be at any of them.

Despite her wariness of her own employer, she'd then contacted a friend of hers, Gavril, who worked in the cyber crimes unit, for any updates about Elias and the Americans' whereabouts; her gut told her Stavros' disappearance was linked somehow. He promised he'd subtly check and get back to her.

She'd thought about contacting Yiannis directly for updates on the case. They were friendly, and while she wasn't nearly as close with him as she was with Stavros, she respected him, and they got along. But given his appearance in her hospital room with Tobias, whom she was incredibly suspicious of, she'd decided against it. She couldn't risk it if he were being monitored. She just had to do something; her worry was like a constant adrenaline rush, forcing her to remain in motion. The only place she hadn't gone was to his office at police headquarters; something told her that was the last place she should go. She'd only slept for a couple of hours before coming to see Helena, whom she also considered a good friend, hoping to get some insight into what Stavros had been looking into.

"I could barely get the kids off to school this morning. I haven't told them anything, yet, just that their father's away. I just—I don't want to think—"

"Hey," Athena said gently, squeezing her hand. "I'm going to find him. And when I do, I'm going to kick his ass for scaring us both so much." She smiled, and Helena wiped her tears, returning her smile, though it was forced. "I know you've already spoken to his boss, but I need you to tell me anything Stavros might have told you about what he was looking into. Anything, however small, could help."

"Well," Helena said, after a brief pause, "I didn't tell the police this—something told me not to. A couple of weeks ago, Stavros became increasingly paranoid. He insisted on picking up the girls from school when he could. He even asked me if I'd noticed anyone following us. When I asked him what was going on, he told me he thought his department was compromised in some way. He refused to give me any more details, said he needed to find out more information. He made me swear not to tell anyone." Helena closed her eyes, guilt flickering across her expression. "I should have pressed harder. I should have insisted that he—"

"None of this your fault," Athena insisted.

"I was going to reach out to you, right before you texted," Helena said. "I—"

Rapid knocks on the front door interrupted her, and they both stiffened.

Athena stood, her instincts kicking in as she reached for her service weapon. "Get the door," she said in a low voice. "I'll hide. If you have any trouble—"

"I know," Helena said shakily. "I trust you."

Athena made her way to the living room closet, pressing herself inside as Helena went to answer the door. The words were muffled from where she stood, but she soon heard footsteps as several people entered the home.

Athena cautiously cracked open the door. Men wearing Hellenic Police uniforms entered, carrying empty boxes, making their way up the stairs. She knew where they were going—to Stavros' office.

She remained hidden until they came down minutes later, carrying boxes filled with paperwork, ignoring Helena's demand for answers. Athena waited for another several minutes before emerging from the closet after they left.

"They told me they needed to look into Stavros' records to help with their investigation," Helena said, frowning with suspicion.

"I'm going to get to the bottom of this," Athena promised. "In the meanwhile, I don't want to scare you, but—"

"I'm going to take the girls out of school today and go to my mother's in Chalcis," Helena said immediately.

Athena nodded, satisfied. "I'll be in touch."

"Stay safe," Helena said, giving her a hug. "And Athena . . . bring him home."

CHAPTER 21

Dikti Mountain Range
Crete
2:32 P.M.

Adrian reached the summit of the mountain, right after Myia, with Nick and Elias arriving behind her.

She took in the stunning vistas that surrounded them, mountain peaks arching toward the clear blue sky, looming over green hills and verdant plateaus below. With the peaks lit by fires at night, the views must have been breathtaking in ancient times. She could imagine the Minoans using this area as a sacred place for religious rites; it seemed as if it were literally on top of the world—and close to the gods.

The climb hadn't been as grueling as she'd feared. The ascent was indeed a gradual one; it had been more like taking a long hike. While there had been some rocky sections to maneuver, they didn't need to use any of their rope equipment. They'd been able to easily make their way up, even Elias. They'd only taken a break twice to rest and eat the sandwiches they'd bought at the sporting goods store before continuing.

There were a couple of times during the trek that Adrian had felt as if she were being watched; she'd even stopped, taken out her binoculars and scanned her surroundings. Myia and Nick did the same, but they had seen no one else on the trail with them. It must have been her nerves working in overdrive after what happened in Heraklion. Still, the sensation had increased her urgency to get to the peak.

During the climb, Myia was quietly hostile toward Elias, glaring at him but never addressing him directly. Nick was less hostile, but still wary around him. As for Adrian, she was more trusting of Elias than the others, but she was still watching him closely for any sign of further deception.

Elias, for his part, said nothing unless spoken to, and pretended not to notice Myia's glares and Nick's obvious suspicion. She knew it would take time for any sort of trust to form among the group again, or if it ever would during the time they were working together.

While Nick and Elias were finishing up their sandwiches, Myia moved away from the group to look out at the plateaus below the mountain peaks. Adrian joined her, and they stood in silence for several long moments.

"Ben—Socrates—and I would sometimes go hiking around here. Away from the popular tourist trails," Myia said. "He actually wanted to be a mountain guide once upon a time, before he got into the antiquities business. He told me he only really felt at peace in nature."

"I'm sorry about what happened to him," Adrian said. "Truly."

"We were dating, actually. It wasn't serious—yet. He was the one who wanted more. I always held back. Now, I wish I'd . . . " Her voice trailed off, and she blinked back tears. "I learned you should never take for granted what's right in front of you." She gave Adrian a knowing look, her gaze sliding to Nick, before she walked away, consulting her map.

Adrian stilled at her words. During her time working with Nick these past few months, their friendship had deepened, and Adrian could no longer deny her attraction to her partner. But she didn't want to upset the renewed friendship and bond they'd formed after so many years of being apart. Yet she couldn't deny the truth of Myia's words. She and Nick were constantly facing danger. How would she feel if something happened to him and she'd never let him know of her growing feelings?

Adrian had put aside her turbulent emotions as they'd continued their trek up the mountain, though her gaze continually strayed to Nick, Myia's words echoing in her mind.

"The area we need to get to is slightly to the west," Myia said now, looking down at her map.

They trailed Myia westward, making their way down a slope until they reached a cave that jutted out from the side of the mountain, surrounded by a rocky outcrop.

"This has to be it," Myia said, the excitement transparent in her tone as they took in the cave.

They ventured forward, heading into a spacious cave. Adrian turned, beaming her flashlight around the interior. She froze, noticing a horizontal opening tucked away at the base of the rear cave wall.

"Guys," she said, approaching it. She knelt, shining her flashlight into the crevasse. It opened up to a slightly wider passageway. It would be a tight squeeze, but she'd be able to maneuver her way through it.

"I don't know," Nick hedged. "How do you even know if anything's on the other side? You could just end up trapped."

"We've come all this way. What if there's something there?" Adrian pressed.

"I can go instead," Myia offered. "I'm the smallest of the group."

"I'm coming as well," Adrian insisted. While

taller than Myia, she was slender enough to make her way through the crevasse.

"Don't try to argue with her," Nick warned Myia. "You'll never win. This woman puts the S in stubborn."

"I don't know what you're talking about," Adrian protested with a playful grin.

Nick eyed the space warily, heaving a sigh. He reached out, giving her a hand a squeeze. "Be careful, all right, West?"

"Always," she said, her hand lingering in his for a moment before she stepped away.

Strapping on her headlamp and dropping her backpack, Adrian crawled onto her belly and wriggled her way into the narrow crawlspace.

Adrian wasn't claustrophobic, but as soon as she entered and could see nothing but blackness, panic tugged at the edges of her senses. She took a calming breath and continued to make her way forward. She soon heard Myia enter behind her, and now felt grateful that someone else was with her.

After what felt like an eternity, though it was likely only a few minutes, she spotted a faint shaft of light up ahead. She crawled toward it and emerged into another open area. It was decidedly smaller than the main area of the cave, roughly seven feet tall and twelve feet wide.

She stilled as her headlamp illuminated the space, and she spotted something on the far wall.

Behind her, she heard Myia gasp as she emerged from the crawlspace behind her.

A massive petroglyph of a labyrinth filled the expanse of the rear wall. In the very center of the labyrinth, was the same pre-Greek word found on Solon's papyrus, and the inscription on the shards, written in the Linear A script.

Atai. The ancient word for Atlantis.

CHAPTER 22

3:17 P.M.

Myia, Nick, and Elias stood next to Adrian, shining their flashlights at the petroglyph, taking it in with silent awe.

After she and Myia had made the discovery, they'd shouted for Nick and Elias, who'd taken the risk of making their way through the narrow crawlspace to the area of the cave they now stood in. They'd already taken multiple photos of the symbol with their phones, and now just stared at it, still not quite believing what was before them.

Elias stepped forward, shaking his head in disbelief. "Writing on cave walls in this region is incredibly rare. This is the first I've seen."

"What could this mean?" Myia asked. In light of the discovery, her hostility toward Elias had temporarily dissipated.

"The labyrinth symbol has mysterious origins. We're not quite certain where the word itself came from, but it's very old—from a pre-Greek language. The symbol appears on coins going back to antiquity. And it's not just been found in Europe, but all over the world, from the Americas to Australia. During the ancient Greek period, it was typically associated with the underground. By medieval times, it had taken on the form of what we now think of as a maze. As for the meaning, that can vary, and there are many theories. Some theorize it just means a place that can hold a monster—"

"Like the Minotaur myth," Nick interjected.

"Yes. With the Minotaur typically being depicted in the center," Elias said.

Adrian mulled over Elias' words, wondering what further significance they could glean from the labyrinth symbol.

"I know you can't date this symbol without equipment, but what time period would you guess this is from? Who would have been here and carved this?" she asked Elias.

"By the style of the writing and the petroglyph itself, I would guesstimate that this was made around the time of the fall of the Minoan civilization—around 1200 BCE, during the time of the late Bronze Age collapse, during which many ancient civilizations came to an abrupt end. As for who made this . . . it was likely done by Minoan refugees, forced to flee their homes because of invasion. There have been finds in caves all around

Crete that have led archaeologists to believe that some Minoans made their last stand on the outskirts of their former civilization before they were ultimately conquered by the Mycenaean Greeks. I think that's why Socrates found the shards here, and why we've found this. Put yourselves into their mind space," Elias continued, shining his light over the petroglyph. "They're about to lose their home to invaders. They're losing the war, but they're desperate."

"So they make a prayer to their gods," Adrian said, thinking of the inscription on the shards. "For them to write this symbol down—and this old word for Atlantis..."

"It had to be important," Nick added.

"And," Elias added, after a brief pause, "there's another possible meaning of the labyrinth symbol."

"What?" Adrian asked.

"Origin." He again shined his light onto the labyrinth, highlighting the circular paths it made to the center. "With the paths of the labyrinth leading to that origin—it could be of the ancestor. Home."

"So you're saying that Atlantis . . . " Myia hedged.

"Could have been their original home. Long lost to them by then, but still, an origin that was in their shared memory. A place to return to now that the home they'd made for themselves was on the verge of being lost," Elias murmured, his tone reverent in the hushed silence of the cave.

They met each other's eyes, reeling at the

implication of Elias' words, when a loud, male voice boomed out from the other side of the cave.

"Unless you want to die in there, I'd advise that you all come out now."

CHAPTER 23

3:47 P.M.

Adrian emerged from the crawlspace that led back out to the main area of the cave, panic clogging her throat as she got to her feet.

The young police officer from the station in Hersonissos, Lucas Dimou, along with another man she didn't recognize, stood there. Lucas' expression was hard as he aimed his service weapon at her. He must have been the one to help Michalis escape. She now recalled the sense she had of being followed and wanted to kick herself. Her instincts had been right. They should have been more careful, more watchful.

The men stood by the entrance to the cave, blocking their only escape, their weapons leveled at her chest. Shaking, Adrian held up her hands, remaining still as Nick, Myia, and Elias emerged behind her.

She swallowed, her eyes going to the packs by the door where their weapons were. They were cornered and unarmed.

"You're going to tell us what you found here," Lucas said, turning to aim his gun at Myia. "Or I'm going to start killing your friends, one by one."

"A petroglyph of a labyrinth symbol," Adrian said without hesitation. "You can check our phones. They're in our pockets."

Lucas raised his eyebrows, looking surprised at her quick acquiescence. He nodded to the man at his side. "Vasilis. Check her," he ordered in Greek.

As Vasilis approached, Adrian sized him up. He was her height but solidly built; she would have to move fast. Her heart thudded in a haphazard rhythm in her ears, but she did her best to appear outwardly calm.

She slid a subtle glance to Nick and knew with that one look he was aware of her intentions. They were so in sync that he always seemed to know.

As soon as Vasilis got close, Adrian made her move. She lunged forward, headbutting him. He stumbled back, startled and gripping his head, as Nick and Myia darted forward.

Nick charged Lucas, who lifted his arm to fire his weapon. Nick reached him just in time, yanking his arm upward to point at the ceiling of the cave, where the bullet ricocheted. He then tackled Lucas to the ground as Adrian kicked Vasilis in the groin, sending him to his knees. He let out a snarl of rage and pain, reaching up to yank her down as well.

Her head hit the solid ground of the cave, hard, and as pain careened through her temple, Vasilis straddled her, raising his weapon—

A gunshot rang out. Vasilis went still above her as the bullet struck him, clutching his chest before slumping over.

Adrian rolled out from beneath him, her head still throbbing with pain. She looked up; Myia stood just behind Vasilis, lowering her gun.

Myia and Elias helped her to her feet as Adrian turned her focus to Nick, who was wrestling Lucas for his gun.

They raced toward them. Adrian stepped on Lucas' shin, hard, until she heard the sickening crack of bone. Lucas howled, jerking back in pain, giving Nick a temporary advantage. He yanked the gun from Lucas, getting to his feet. Myia rushed forward, aiming her weapon at Lucas' head.

"Who are you working for?" Adrian demanded, glaring at Lucas.

"I'm not telling you anything, bitch," Lucas snarled.

"I'd think very carefully about how you talk to us now that we have the upper hand," Nick growled.

"Whatever they're paying you, we can pay you more," Adrian said, hoping that would appeal to Lucas' mercenary side.

Lucas spat out a bitter laugh. "Some things are worth more than money," he hissed. "The ancient wisdom will prevail. Destruction will cause salvation."

Unease slithered through her at his words, which all but seemed to confirm that whomever he was working for was seeking a weapon with this "ancient wisdom."

"What do you mean by that?" she pressed.

Lucas just glared. Adrian heaved a sigh, taking a step back. He wasn't going to talk—yet. They needed to get him into custody, but this time, they needed to make sure whomever he was working for didn't get to him like they had with Michalis.

She looked at Nick. "We need to—" she began.

In a rapid movement, Lucas abruptly reached up, twisting Myia's hand, who stumbled back with a cry of pain, forcing her to drop her gun. Lucas picked up the discarded weapon, raising it to fire at Adrian.

But Nick was faster, shooting him in the chest. Lucas fell backward, his body going still.

Nick approached her, his face pale with fear. "You OK?"

"I'm fine," she said, giving him a reassuring smile.

But Nick still looked shaken. "I thought—" He trailed off, an unreadable emotion passing over his features as he swallowed hard.

Adrian reached out to squeeze his hands, taking comfort in the rush of warmth that filled her at his touch. "You're not getting soft on me, are you?" she murmured. "I've faced worse."

"Don't remind me," Nick grunted, but gave her a smile that caused even more heat to flare up in her chest.

"Elias and I are both fine, by the way," Myia said drily, wincing as she rubbed at her hand. "And this is touching and all, but we need to get the hell out of here. These two bastards may have backup on the way."

CHAPTER 24

Malia, Crete
7:52 P.M.

"Here we are," Myia said. "What's that expression you have in America? Home sweet home."

Myia turned, giving them a wry smile. They were all still shaken from the confrontation in the cave, but they returned her smile.

They had just arrived at Myia's home, a ramshackle beach house on the outskirts of the coastal town of Malia. Before leaving the mountain, they'd had no choice but to contact Briggs on his secure line at the bureau to tell him what happened since they'd last spoken. They'd taken Lucas' phone, which appeared to be a burner with only one number on it. They'd given the number to Briggs, who'd promised to have Vince and Jonathan run a trace.

"I'll send someone to deal with this Lucas Dimou and his henchman," Briggs assured them. "Just get yourselves to safety. I'll also get Vince and Jonathan to run background, see what they can find out about Dimou. Update me later when, and if, you can."

"There's something else," Adrian said, and told them her theory that Lucas'—and Michalis'—employer was searching for a weapon with the ruins of Atlantis, and how Lucas' words seemed to confirm her theory.

Briggs swore under his breath, but repeated what Adrian had already concluded. "Then we're just going to have to get there first. I'll reach out to other agencies, see if they have any intel on a weapon these bastards are looking for."

They'd hiked down the mountain to a village Myia had pointed out on her map, where they paid a local driver to take them to their rental truck. Adrian had been on edge during the entire journey, keeping track of their surroundings to make certain they weren't still being followed. It still unnerved her that Lucas had tracked them so successfully. And whoever Lucas was working for would soon know they'd gone to the cave; she had no doubt that he'd told them about it. It was only a matter of time before they discovered the petroglyph.

Myia led them to the front door. Rather than using a key, Myia entered a code into a keypad just below the doorknob. The door swung open to reveal a surprisingly modern and upscale interior, which was at odds with the ramshackle exterior.

"I renovated the interior but purposefully kept the exterior shabby. In my line of work, it's best to appear as . . . humble as possible," Myia said with a rueful grin, taking in their startled expressions. "Stay here. I'm going to make sure it's secure."

Myia left them in the foyer as she headed farther inside. She returned moments later, gesturing for them to follow her into a dining room.

"I don't have much to eat, just noodles and water," she said apologetically, as she headed into the adjoining kitchen.

Adrian watched her go, realizing how significant it was that Myia had brought them to her home.

Myia had told them her home was difficult to find. It wasn't in her real name, and she'd taken great pains to keep where she lived private; they'd be safe there for now. Myia hadn't trusted them an inch when they'd first come across each other, and she knew Myia was still wary of Elias, though she'd seemed to soften a little toward him since the events in the cave—he had helped them after all. Given that they'd narrowly escaped two near-death encounters since their meeting, Adrian wondered if that automatically brought about this trust.

"What happened in that cave proves the police are involved," Nick said grimly, after Myia returned with bowls of hot noodles and bottles of water.

Adrian nodded her agreement. Were other police departments in Crete infiltrated? Which ones? And if so, whom could they trust?

Her thoughts turned back to the petroglyph of the labyrinth they'd discovered in the cave, and the old word for Atlantis.

"You mentioned that one meaning of the labyrinth symbol could mean home," she said to Elias, "which could mean that Atlantis was the original home of whoever drew that symbol on the cave wall."

"I've thought more about that during the drive here, and there's a problem with my conjecture," Elias said, heaving a sigh. "We know from genetic evidence, the Minoans originated from Anatolia, which is modern-day Turkey—not Atlantis."

"Well, we don't know that somewhere in Anatolia isn't Atlantis. No one knows exactly where the actual Atlantis could be," Adrian argued. "And maybe their origin goes back even further. You also mentioned the Bronze Age collapse in the cave—the complete disintegration of multiple advanced societies."

"Yes. From the Minoans to the Hittites to the Babylonians. Even Egypt was affected, growing considerably weaker during this period," Elias said with a grim nod.

"What caused it?" Nick asked.

"No one knows for sure, but it's commonly assumed that a variety of factors contributed to the collapse—climate change, which caused famine, which then caused invasions by the mysterious so-called Sea Peoples—and warfare," Elias replied.

"It took time for all those advanced societies to evolve, and after the collapse, those societies fell into a dark age," Adrian said slowly. "What if we were to go back even further in time . . . to the dawn of these advanced societies? What if they have a common origin?"

"To Atlantis?" Myia proposed.

"To Atlantis," Adrian confirmed. "Maybe the original founders of these societies could build new settlements based on their knowledge of their homeland, an advanced ancient society they originated from. During the time of the Bronze Age collapse, what if there was some ancient, shared memory they had of their long-lost homeland, represented through the symbol of the labyrinth and an old word for their homeland, Atai. They inscribe it onto cave walls, libation vessels. It's just like we proposed in the cave. A longing to return to their old home as their new one collapsed around them."

Elias, Nick, and Myia were silent, but she could tell they were weighing her words.

"We have the Solon papyrus, the inscriptions on the shard, and now the petroglyph we found in that cave, all referring to Atlantis. But we need more. Something concrete. This is still all just speculation. We're still no closer to discovering a potential location for Atlantis," Adrian said with a sigh of frustration.

"Ironically, you know what would be helpful now?" Nick asked with an amused chuckle. "One of those labyrinths that people walk through when they need to come up with ideas."

They all turned to look at him. Nick's smile faded, and he raised his eyebrows.

"What?"

∼

9:04 P.M.

Adrian walked through one of the makeshift labyrinths that Myia and Elias had drawn into the sand behind the beach house. Lit only by moonlight, it gave the labyrinth an almost magical appearance. She wondered if the ancients had also used the symbol in such a way as well, making their way around the twisting patterns to the center as they'd contemplated.

They had taken Nick's playful suggestion to heart. "It can't hurt," Myia said with a shrug. "And God knows we need ideas."

Adrian had to admit that there was something calming about making her way through the paths of the ancient symbol. It forced her to concentrate on what was directly ahead of her, centering her focus.

Opposite her, Nick had already made it to the center of his own labyrinth. He was seated there, staring out at the restless waters, his brow furrowed the way it did whenever he was in deep concentration. Elias was still making his way through the labyrinth he'd drawn for himself, looking deep in thought as well. Behind them, Myia was seated cross-legged on the sand, a beer in her hand as she watched them.

"I'm more of an action person. I'll let you academic types do the hard thinking," she'd said with a chuckle.

"Are you calling us nerds?" Nick asked, with a look of mock offense. "Adrian, I think she just called us nerds."

Adrian turned her thoughts back to the present, continuing to make her way toward the center of the labyrinth. She thought of Solon's papyrus, the inscriptions on the shards, the petroglyph in the cave. As she reached the center of the labyrinth, she again thought of the word Atlantis itself in the pre-Greek language. *Atai*. She looked down at the center of the labyrinth, where she now stood. *Home*.

Gazing out at the glittering, dark waters of the Bay of Malia, Adrian recalled a tidbit Elias had told her about peak sanctuaries, how they were built to be seen from other mountain peaks throughout Crete. She focused on a distant point on the horizon, to where the Greek isles lay to the north, and beyond that, continental Europe. She turned her body to face the east, where Turkey—then called Anatolia—lay.

She froze as a possible solution hit her. Could it really be that simple?

"I know that look, West," Nick called over to her.

Adrian turned to face them. Nick was staring at her expectantly. Myia got to her feet, and Elias stepped out of his labyrinth to approach her.

"I think I know how we can find their original homeland," she said. "How we can find Atlantis."

CHAPTER 25

Hellenic Police Headquarters
Athens, Greece
9:17 P.M.

Athena sat opposite Yiannis, reeling in shock at his words. He was still speaking, but she couldn't hear him over the pounding of her heartbeat, a staccato drumbeat in her ears. She could only hear on repeat what he'd told her as soon as she'd entered his office after he'd summoned her.

Stavros' body has been found—in his car, on the outskirts of Athens. It was a single gunshot wound to the head. Suicide. No foul play. His family's been notified. I wanted to tell you myself. I'm so sorry, Athena.

Athena's head began to pound, and nausea rose. She forced it down, raising her eyes to meet

Yiannis'. He was leaning forward in his chair, looking at her with concern, and she realized he'd been saying her name.

"I'm so sorry. I know you two were close. Is there anyone I can call?"

Athena wanted to laugh. Stavros was the only person she would have called. She'd broken up with her longtime partner years ago because of her workaholic tendencies. Her parents were long dead, she had no siblings or close friends, and she wasn't close to her extended family. Her whole life had been her work, and as a result, her only family was Stavros.

Her only family was now dead.

Athena got to her feet, blinking back tears. She wouldn't cry here, not in front of Yiannis.

"It wasn't suicide," she muttered.

Yiannis' expression shifted to one that was unreadable. He straightened in his seat. "Athena, you—"

Athena turned and stumbled out of his office, ignoring him as he called after her. She felt the eyes of other police officers on her face as she hurried out of the station. She must have looked a sight: pale-faced and shell-shocked, fighting back nausea and tears. The nausea continued to rise, so much so that she vomited in the trash can just outside the building.

She wiped her mouth and closed her eyes. All she could see in her mind's eye were her times with

Stavros. The cases they worked together, the long hours of stakeouts, interviews, and investigations. The laughter and the friendship.

From her shock and grief, anger emerged, filling her with such force that she began to shake. She made herself think . . . and a realization dawned. *Of course.* She should have looked at what was in front of her this whole time.

Athena hurried to her car, taking the familiar route by heart without even thinking about it. She parked outside of Stavros' home, now dark since Helena and the kids had left for her mother's.

Helena and the kids. Athena's heart swelled with grief. If she was this devastated, she could only imagine how Helena felt. She would reach out to Helena later, but for now, she needed to find the asshole who'd murdered her best friend.

She got out of her car, looking around to make certain she wasn't being followed or that anyone was lurking, before using the spare key to unlock the door and head inside.

Athena made her way to Stavros' office. She'd realized she needed to retrace her steps, to go back to the simplest point of origin, something she did in all her investigations. Stavros was an expert at hiding things. He had a habit of pranking her by hiding her keys in the office, or hiding some work file she was poring over, his way of forcing her to go home whenever she worked too hard. He always went out of his way to take care of her.

She closed her eyes, fighting back tears. Stavros would think the safest place would be his home, but he wouldn't leave anything in plain sight, and those officers who were here the other day had taken his things.

Taking a breath, Athena looked around. Where would Stavros hide something? She started by looking under things—the desk, the couch, the chairs. When nothing came up, frustration coursed through her... until she looked up.

She scanned the ceiling and froze when she saw it. There, in the far corner, one of the ceiling panels looked slightly loose. She grabbed a chair and stood on top of it, pushing on the panel. It lifted, and a small box fell out, tumbling to the floor.

She opened it. Inside, there was a burner phone. Shaking, she took out the phone, relieved to see that it was fully charged. She looked at the call log, dialing the very last number called.

A cheerful female voice answered via automatic message.

"Welcome to the offices of CHSR, the Center of Historical and Scientific Research."

Malia, Crete
9:36 P.M.

NICK, Myia, and Elias hovered as Adrian rolled out a map of Crete, the Aegean, and the Mediterranean, on the dining room table. Adrian had noticed Myia's collection of maps in her dining room, and Myia had provided Adrian with one at her request.

"Elias, you said that from genetic evidence, we know the ancient Cretans came from Anatolia," Adrian said.

"Yes. Central then later northwest Anatolia," Elias confirmed.

"So we know they migrated from there. You also mentioned that peak sanctuaries were situated so that they could be visible from other mountain peaks," she continued. Elias gave her a nod of confirmation. "But what if there's more to it? What if the peak sanctuaries served as directional waypoints? We may not know much about Minoan religion, but it was heavy with symbolism."

"You're saying that the sanctuaries built on mountain peaks pointed in a certain direction?" Elias asked.

"Yes. I think that the peak sanctuary we found was pointing toward what these peoples believed to be their original home," Adrian replied.

"It's certainly possible," Elias said after a brief pause. "Ancient peoples used many types of directional signposts in the days before maps."

"I assume you're familiar with peak sanctuaries in the area?" she asked Elias. "Can you mark them off on the map?"

She picked up a pack of sticky notes that Myia

had also provided. Elias stepped forward, placing down the notes on a half-dozen peak and cave sanctuary sites around Crete.

"These are the ones I know by heart—the museum's taken in artifacts from these sites," Elias said. He added the last note to the peak sanctuary they'd just come from.

"Can you find other peak sanctuary sites in the archaeological database you have access to?" she asked Elias.

An hour later, they stood behind Myia's computer screen, looking at a map of Crete and the surrounding islands and landmasses. Myia had placed digital markers of peak and cave sanctuaries all over Crete and some of the surrounding islands, using Elias' input.

"Well, I'll be damned," Nick murmured.

The sanctuary sites seemed to point north, toward the eastern shores of Turkey . . . Anatolia, during the time of the Minoans.

Myia didn't look as impressed. "It's not specific enough. They could be pointing at any location in Turkey, or even farther north than that."

"I don't think so," Elias murmured. "Zoom in on Ikaria." He pointed to an island in the North Aegean Sea.

Myia obliged. Elias grinned as he took it in.

"What are you seeing?" Nick asked.

"While it seems like these peaks are pointing in the general direction of Anatolia, I think they are pointing to a specific place—the one on Ikaria confirms this. It may have even been visible to the locals of Ikaria in ancient times." He turned to face them. "One of the most famous ancient cities in the world, one that was very recently assumed to be myth. Troy."

CHAPTER 26

"Troy," Nick echoed. "As in *The Odyssey*? The Trojan horse and all that? You're saying that's Atlantis?"

"I'm saying that's where the peak sanctuaries seem to point to," Elias said. "Troy was once thought to be nothing more than myth until its archaeological remains were discovered and excavations began in the nineteenth century."

"What do you know about the historical Troy?" Adrian asked.

"Troy was inhabited for around eight thousand years. It was the crossroads between Anatolia, the Aegean and Balkan civilizations. It most definitely influenced Homer's *The Iliad* and Virgil's *Aeneid*. There's been debate as to the accuracy of Homer's description of the Trojan War, but some historians place it around the time of the Bronze Age collapse."

Adrian leaned back, considering this. Was Troy

connected to Atlantis? Or could Troy possibly be Atlantis itself?

"There have been theories about Troy being Atlantis," Elias said, giving her a knowing look. "One of the main arguments is the same argument one could make about any advanced ancient civilization during this time period—a maritime power that came to a catastrophic end. But we know from the Bronze Age collapse that multiple societies fell in similar ways. While I don't think Troy is Atlantis, I think it might hold some answers for us and lead us in the right direction. I have a contact who works at the archaeological site who we could talk to," Elias offered.

"No. We don't trust your contacts," Myia said immediately. Her hostility toward Elias had dimmed, but now seemed to flare up again. She glared at him. "Your last *contact* tried to kill us."

"She has a point," Nick said, his eyes narrowing.

Adrian studied Elias. Though she was less wary than the others and didn't believe that Elias would betray them again, she was still on edge after Lucas had tracked them. She didn't know how far his mysterious employer's reach went.

"To be cautious, we'll wait until we get closer to the site to reach out to your contact," she said. She turned to Myia and Nick. "You guys know we're going to need all the help we can get on this."

Myia scowled, but Nick gave her a grudging nod.

Adrian looked down at the map, studying the area near the coast of Turkey that showed the archaeological site of ancient Troy, wondering if that was where they would find the crucial link to Atlantis—before this mysterious organization did.

Knossos, Crete
11:17 P.M.

STEPHANOS STOOD before the Knossos Palace complex, only half listening as his personal historical expert droned on about its history and design. With his connections, he'd been granted access to the site even at the late hour.

His gaze shifted to the ruins. He stood before one of the main buildings, its red pillars standing proudly before faded frescoes. Though the complex was now merely a mass of crumbling stonework and reconstructed frescoes, there was still a sense of the magnificence of what this complex must have looked like at the height of the Minoan civilization. He'd been here countless times, and as an appreciator of history, awe had always swept over him at the sight. Now he felt nothing but impatience. His expert was telling him everything he'd heard before.

Since arriving in Crete, he'd been to all three of the Minoan palaces with his expert, hoping to gain some new information that could point toward Atlantis, but he'd learned nothing new.

A fresh wave of anger coursed through him at the thought of Elias with Adrian West and her partner. His men had gone after the traitor's family, but they'd disappeared, likely taken into protective custody by the Americans. Elias and West could be way ahead of him by now.

Irina approached, holding up her phone. She'd insisted on coming with him, telling him he needed loyal allies at his side, and promising she'd be able to carry out her investigation even as she traveled with him.

"It's—Dmitris," she said, giving him a cautious look. "I tried to hold him off, but—"

"It's fine," he said shortly, taking her phone.

The board members of CHSR had been hounding him, wanting to know his progress, but he'd evaded them, telling him he'd reach out in due time. He knew it was only so long that he could evade them, so he reluctantly took the call.

Stephanos took a breath before answering, reminding himself to keep his calm. He knew Dmitris was working against him. If he kept that in mind, he could hold rein in his temper—for now. He would get his revenge. He just needed patience.

"Why haven't you been answering our calls?" Dmitris barked as soon as Stephanos answered. "We've all been trying to reach you. I heard about what happened in Heraklion. Are you in Crete right now?"

"Yes. I have reason to believe there may be something that points to Atlantis at one of the Minoan palaces," Stephanos replied shortly.

Dmitris scoffed. "We've looked into the Minoan connection countless times over the years."

"I know that," Stephanos said through gritted teeth. "I wanted to—"

He stopped himself. He didn't have to explain himself to this *maláka*.

"I have to go," he bit out instead. "I assure you that everything is being taken care of."

"It doesn't sound like it," Dmitris snapped. "The others and I have been talking. We're thinking of having someone else from the organization take this over. Fresh eyes can bring new perspective. We've appreciated everything you've done, but we think it's time for you to step aside."

Rage filled his veins, and Stephanos clenched his fists. He stepped away from Irina and the expert, both of whom were pretending to not listen to his side of the conversation, lowering his voice to a threatening growl.

"You and I both know you would be nothing without my father—and now me. You need to be very careful about threatening me. I'm no fool, Dmitris. I know you and your idiot son are trying to work against me. You will fail. And you will regret ever trying to stop me."

Stephanos hung up, glaring down at the phone. He should have known he would lose his temper. It was foolish to reveal that he knew Dmitris was working against him, but his complete lack of denial was all the proof he needed.

Still, Dmitris' threat unnerved him. He would need to again reach out to his allies to make certain they were still behind him.

His phone shrilled again, and he stiffened when he saw that it was Tobias. He almost didn't want to answer, fearing it was more bad news.

"Setback or progress?" he asked as soon as he answered.

"Progress," Tobias said, his voice wavering with excitement. "We lost some of our men—looks like they got into a confrontation with those American agents. But they found something at a cave in Crete, and I'm looking at it right now. A labyrinth symbol. Another link to Atlantis."

CHAPTER 27

Troy Archaeological Site
Hisarlik, Çanakkale Province, Turkey
10:07 A.M.

Early that morning, Adrian and the others flew from Heraklion International Airport to Izmir Adnan Menderes Airport in Turkey, where they'd taken a rental car to the archaeological site of ancient Troy. There, they were to meet Dilara Aydin, an archaeologist friend of Elias' who worked at the site.

It wasn't until they were on their way to the site from the airport that they'd allowed Elias to contact Dilara, making him place the call on speaker. To his credit, Elias hadn't complained, dutifully telling her their cover story, that he was with three professor friends who were in Izmir for an academic conference, and that they'd love a brief, personal tour of the site. To her relief, Dilara, who sounded both surprised and happy to hear from Elias, had readily agreed, though she told him she only had an hour or two to spare.

After they parked and approached the entrance to the site, Adrian chuckled when she saw the wooden Trojan horse that loomed there, representing one of the most popular scenes from the myth in which soldiers from the opposing side of the war snuck into Troy by hiding in a horse gifted to the city.

Dilara, a slender, attractive brunette, soon approached them. Elias stepped forward to introduce them while Adrian and the others regarded her; they were all wary after the incident with Kostas. But unlike Kostas, there was no unease in Dilara's body language. She seemed nothing but friendly and open. Still, Adrian kept her guard up as they trailed her down the wooden boardwalk that wound its way around the ruins for tourists to use.

"The site as a whole consists of roughly nine layers of settlement, built on top of each other over the course of thousands of years. The sixth layer was believed to be the Troy of Homer. It fit the description of Homer's Troy; it was right next to the Aegean and the Dardanelles Strait, along with Mount Ida," Dilara said. "Given the defensive fortifications found, it's likely that battles were fought at Troy during this time period—excavations have also unearthed weapons."

Dilara pointed out the fortified citadel where

the wealthy inhabitants had lived, and the area outside the citadel where the lower classes lived. She then led them to a section where excavators had marked out the layers of the site, indicating the multiple layers of the civilization of Troy, designated as Troy I to Troy VII.

"What else can you tell us about the sixth layer?" Adrian asked. "What type of artifacts have been found there?"

"They mostly consist of pottery or copper artifacts from various cultures, showing what a crossroads this region was. It had cultural ties to Northwest Anatolia, not as much from other regions. Evidence tells us it was likely destroyed by an earthquake, but it could also have come to its end by war. The layer above it, Troy VII, was completely destroyed during the Bronze Age collapse."

"Any inscriptions?" Elias asked. "Maybe excavated from one of the older layers? Engravings or depictions?"

"The only writing that's been found at the site was a bronze seal inscribed in Luwian, an Anatolian language. It hasn't been deciphered except for the word 'scribe,'" Dilara said. She studied them, a look of puzzlement crossing her features. "Is there something specific you're looking for?"

Adrian exchanged a glance with the others. Her gut told her that Dilara genuinely had no idea what they were really looking for, but hadn't she been wrong about Elias? Myia looked wary and gave a subtle shake of her head while Elias' expression remained neutral. It was Nick who made her decision for her; he offered her a nod and a look of reassurance.

"Can you tell us," Adrian said, turning back to Dilara, "what you know about Atlantis?"

CHAPTER 28

Troy Museum
Tevfikiye, Turkey
1:39 P.M.

The Troy Museum, where many of the finds excavated from the archaeological site were sent, was located in the nearby village of Tevfikiye. Adrian and the others were gathered in one of the records' rooms, combing through stacks of documents Dilara had provided them with.

Adrian told her they were doing a talk on the viable locations for a real-life Atlantis at the academic conference they were attending. Dilara hadn't hidden her skepticism, practically rolling her eyes. "No disrespect to your research, but I don't think Atlantis was real, but a metaphor. There's no conclusive evidence that it existed."

They had remained silent. Though Adrian knew that news of Solon's papyrus had leaked, it was obvious that Dilara didn't know of its existence.

Despite her skepticism, Dilara had humored them, providing them with records of artifacts uncovered from the excavations of the various layers of Troy, even from the surrounding prehistoric cemeteries and settlements. Thus far, they'd found nothing akin to what they'd discovered at the peak sanctuary or anything that would point to a historical Atlantis.

Adrian pushed away one of the files she'd been poring over, wearily rubbing her eyes. She leaned back in her chair. What were they missing? She thought again of the labyrinth symbol and the notion of origin. *Home.* What connected the ancient Minoans to this area?

Taking out her phone, Adrian opened up an encrypted file to study the map they'd used to pinpoint the peak sanctuaries in the region that Myia had sent to her.

"Is there somewhere else the peak sanctuaries could be pointing to?" she asked Elias. "Or is my conjecture completely wrong?"

Adrian handed him her phone, and he studied the map. "Well," he said, after a lengthy pause, "there is Miletus."

"Where's that?" Nick asked.

"It's three hours south of here," Elias replied. "Ancient Greek writers state that it was founded by settlers from Crete, who even named the city after their native home—Miletus. The archaeological record supports this. Artifacts from Minoan civilization have been found there."

"Why would they go there?" Myia asked.

"No one is certain why they settled there, but there are theories—war, disease, famine. The same reason people flee their homelands today. There are legendary stories of Miletus' founding, all centering on a hero named Miletus. In two of these versions, he flees Crete to escape the unwanted advances of King Minos."

"King Minos—the mythological king of the Minoans?" Nick asked.

"Indeed," Elias said. "In one of those versions, Miletus marries the daughter of a king after founding the settlement of Miletus. In yet another version, he's exiled from Crete by King Minos, founds Miletus, and marries the daughter of a river god. What do those stories have in common?"

"Miletus fleeing Crete and founding a city. Forming roots by marrying the daughter of a king or a god," Adrian replied.

Elias nodded. "There're often seeds of truth in legend. These tales are similar to how the Minoans fled their home and settled in at Miletus, likely intermarrying with locals."

"OK," Adrian said, drumming her fingers on the table. "Regardless of their reason for fleeing Crete, why would the Minoans go specifically to the area of Miletus?"

There was silence as they all considered Adrian's question.

"We should go to Miletus, see if there's anything of note there. Something that can connect definitively to Atlantis, and perhaps explain why they went there," Elias proposed. "Unfortunately, I don't have any contacts at the Miletus site."

"I do," Myia said. "If you're willing to talk to my contacts . . . they're not exactly above board."

"Let me guess, more black market dealers?" Nick asked with narrowed eyes.

"What I—and my friends do—is not what you think," Myia returned, giving him a hard look.

"We don't know if—" Nick began.

"Again, we need all the help we can get," Adrian said to Nick. She turned back to Myia. "Can you reach out to them?"

At Myia's nod, Adrian got to her feet and moved to the door. As an archaeologist who worked in this region, perhaps Dilara could tell them more about Miletus, or perhaps she also had a contact at Miletus who could give them more information.

When Adrian reached the door and cracked it open, she froze. A confused-looking Dilara was approaching the records room with two Turkish police officers.

CHAPTER 29

2:26 P.M.

Adrian and Nick raced through the parking lot of the museum, crouched low, with Elias and Myia on their heels.

After Adrian spotted the officers, they'd scrambled out the back exit. They made it to the edge of the parking lot, reaching their rental. Adrian climbed into the driver's seat, immediately starting the car as the others piled in.

Before they'd even closed the doors behind them, she sped out of the parking lot, scanning the rearview mirror to make certain they weren't being followed.

"This was you, wasn't it?" Myia snarled, turning to face Elias once they were on the main road leading away from the museum. "You or Dilara—"

"I was working with criminals who threatened

my life and the lives of my family constantly if I even breathed in the direction of the police. Now I'm linked to them. The last thing I'd want to do is contact the police," Elias snapped.

"How can we trust anything you say?" Myia demanded.

"I believe him. He's not had a chance to contact anyone. And for the record, Dilara looked genuinely confused," Adrian interjected. She'd also wondered how they'd been found, but she truly doubted it was Elias. "I don't think Elias or Dilara had anything to do with it."

Out of the corner of her eye, she saw Elias give her a grateful look. Myia still didn't look convinced.

"Then how did the police know we were here?" Myia asked, still glaring at Elias.

"I hate to interrupt this blame game," Nick said grimly, his gaze trained on the passenger-side mirror. "But there's a police car trailing us several cars back."

Adrian's gaze flew to the rearview mirror, spotting the police car and let out a low curse. She'd just turned onto the highway, and ahead of them was a heavy stream of traffic. Tightening her grip on the steering wheel, she changed lanes, increasing her speed. The police car changed lanes as well.

Adrian pressed down on the accelerator, weaving around the traffic. The police car's sirens came on, and it accelerated, speeding after them.

She scanned the road ahead. The traffic was thick and would only slow them down.

Veering abruptly onto the shoulder of the road, Adrian increased her speed until she spotted an off-ramp. She made a sharp left turn, taking the off-ramp and racing onto it. But the police car remained on their tail, and Adrian's heart sank as she spotted another clump of traffic up ahead. As she was about to veer around it—

The police car raced ahead, swerving abruptly in front of her car, blocking her from moving forward.

Two officers emerged, weapons raised, shouting at them in Turkish to get out of the car.

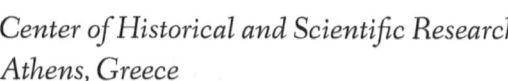

Center of Historical and Scientific Research
Athens, Greece
3:02 P.M.

ATHENA'S MOTHER had named her after the ancient Greek goddess of wisdom. She'd loved Greek mythology and found it fitting to bestow the name upon her daughter. Growing up, Athena had seemed to live up to her moniker, her intellectual curiosity eventually driving her to a career solving crimes, using her problem-solving skills for the better good.

Right now, however, she didn't feel very wise. She sat across from the main campus of the Center of Historical and Scientific Research in a rented van, wearing a blonde wig and dark glasses, studying it through a pair of binoculars.

Ever since discovering the number for the center on Stavros' phone, she had looked into everything she could find about it, but it just seemed to be nothing more than a privately funded scientific research center.

Her gut told her it was much more. She had asked Gavril at headquarters to do some digging for her, off the record, not telling him why. But Gavril had also been a friend of Stavros' and seemed to instinctively know why. He'd promised he'd reach out to her if he found anything, but Athena couldn't sit still, not after what happened to her partner.

She'd decided to come to the main campus of the organization herself to stake it out, though she doubted she would discover anything, and she didn't know what exactly she was looking for. She needed to talk to someone who worked here, to find out exactly what Stavros had been looking into. Right now, she had no basis for a search warrant, given that Stavros' death was officially ruled a suicide, and she was still technically "on leave" from the department.

Athena was starting to wonder if there was a better use of her time, when she spotted a familiar figure leaving the building, his expression stormy. She went absolutely still.

It was Lieutenant Tobias Vasileiou.

CHAPTER 30

Kalafat, Turkey
5:30 P.M.

The police officer slid the jail cell door shut, sealing Adrian and Myia in the cell.

She and Myia were in one cell, while the second officer had taken Nick and Elias to another. They were in a small jail attached to a police station. Unlike the infamous larger prisons in Turkey, it looked as if it were meant to hold drunken locals and unruly tourists, or temporarily hold more dangerous criminals before they were moved to a higher security prison.

That didn't make their predicament any less dangerous. The police officers had claimed they were holding them for the police in Heraklion. She'd feared it was about Lucas and Vasilis after their confrontation in the cave, that Briggs hadn't been able to handle the aftermath, but they'd refused to tell them the reason they were being held, just that the "authorities" wanted to question them. This confirmed for her that their arrest wasn't legitimate, especially when Adrian's and Nick's protests about their status as federal agents had fallen on deaf ears. When Adrian demanded to be put in touch with the American consulate, both officers had only smirked in response.

Adrian turned to Myia. Given Myia's general wariness toward police, she'd expected her to put up much more of a fight. But ever since they'd been taken into custody, the other woman remained eerily quiet. Feeling Adrian's eyes on her, Myia looked up at her and lowered her voice.

"Right before the police caught up to us, I sent a text. I have friends who are going to get us out of here. They are very familiar with how the police here operate."

Adrian stared at her, blinking in surprise. "Friends? Who are they?"

"You're going to have to do what I did for you," Myia responded. "Trust me."

Adrian held her gaze for a moment and gave her a brief nod. She hated feeling so helpless, but at the moment, she had no choice but to trust Myia.

Still, she didn't like being separated from Nick. Even in the most precarious situations she'd found herself in the last few months, she always felt safer when Nick was at her side.

"Your partner is fine," Myia said, as if reading

her mind. She leaned back against the wall, studying her closely. "You two are lovers, no?"

In spite of herself, Adrian felt her cheeks warm, and she was flustered as to a response. Myia chuckled, amused.

"I see. I don't understand why not. I see how he looks at you—and you look at him."

Again, Adrian was at a loss for words. She must not have been great at hiding her growing feelings for Nick. Had he noticed as well? Adrian shook her head as if to clear it. This was ridiculous. At the moment she was in a far more dire predicament than Nick knowing how she felt about him.

"This... help that's coming," she said, deciding to tactfully change the subject. "If they don't get here in time, or if they don't come at all, we're going to have to come up with a plan B."

Myia looked amused at her changing the subject, but played along. "They will come; trust me."

Adrian prayed she was right.

NICK RESTED his head against the wall of his cell, shutting his eyes.

"Well, this is something to check off the old bucket list," he muttered. "Get locked up in a Turkish jail."

He turned to Elias, who sat in the opposite corner, trembling with fear. Despite his lingering distrust toward the man, a stab of sympathy pierced him. Unlike Nick, Adrian, and to a certain extent Myia, he obviously wasn't used to danger like this and was out of his element. It was one reason he was grudgingly starting to agree with Adrian that Elias had been dragged into all of this against his will.

"I should have refused Michalis," Elias said, staring at the floor. "I should have taken my fiancée and ran, warned my family, gone to the police. But then . . . I think about her smile. Lucia is her name. From Italy. She came to Athens to work at the museum because she loves ancient Greece and its history. It's what bonded us. When I proposed, I promised to always love her, protect her." His eyes closed, and he let out a shudder. "When Michalis had her beaten up, I would have done anything—even taken my own life—to keep her safe. Now I don't even know if she is safe, or if the rest of my family—" He trailed off, his voice breaking.

Nick thought of the people he cared about—his sister Elizabeth and her family, and of course, Adrian. Would he do anything in his power to save them if they came under threat? He recalled the fear that had filled him when Lucas had raised his weapon to shoot Adrian. His terror had been . . . visceral. He'd seen Adrian in danger many times before, but this time had felt different. More immediate and real. He didn't know how much longer he could keep his feelings for her to himself. Dread coursed through him at the thought of never getting the chance.

"Hey," he said, and Elias looked at him. "You're human. I would have done the same thing. When we get out of here, and we will, I'll have Briggs confirm that your family is safe, and maybe put you in touch with them."

At the way Elias' eyes lit up, Nick felt a stab of regret for his lingering distrust. His partner, as always, had been right. This was a man whose back had been up against the wall and done what he did to keep his family safe.

The sound of footsteps approaching their cell made him look up. The officer who had locked them in here, a small, stout man, who was in the midst of a massive power trip, sneered down at him.

"The authorities are on their way. But they want answers as to what you've been up to since you left Crete. You're going to give me those answers. If you don't . . . I will have to get answers from those two lovely women you came with. And you won't like the methods I use."

A rush of fury coursed through Nick at his implication. While he knew that Adrian could kick this man's ass, that didn't stop a surge of protectiveness from filling him.

He got to his full height, towering over the officer, giving him a dangerous grin. He had both height and muscle mass over the officer, which was even more apparent now.

"The authorities, huh?" he repeated, knowing

that the officer was full of it. He stepped forward until he was pressed against the bars, only inches away from the officer, who no longer looked smug.

"By all means, question away."

The officer hesitated, swallowing hard. He took a step back, starting to speak, but as he did—

An explosion sounded, rattling the walls and knocking them all backward.

CHAPTER 31

Izmir International Airport
5:58 P.M.

Stephanos studied the photos of the labyrinth inscribed on the cave wall as his private plane made its final descent into Izmir.

After Tobias had informed him of the find, he'd ordered him to send photographs that he could have his experts analyze. As stunning as he found the photos, and as significant of a find that it was, he couldn't help but feel irritated that Elias and the Americans had gotten there first.

But finally, there was some good news, and he let this calm him as he looked out the window.

A contact who worked at the Troy Archaeological Site had spotted Elias, the Americans, and Socrates' girlfriend on a private tour with an archaeologist. It had only taken a few phone calls and a healthy bribe to get the local police to arrest them.

As soon as he'd learned they were in Turkey, he'd had his experts turn their focus to the region to search for possible connections to Atlantis, and they'd come up with several possibilities. He would know if Elias and his colleagues were lying when he interrogated them. And he was looking forward to interrogating them.

Stephanos glanced across the aisle at Irina. After his last conversation with Dmitris, both he and his son had conveniently disappeared; Irina hadn't been able to track them down. The cowards. It had been foolish to tell Dmitris he knew he was working against him, but Irina's lack of progress still irritated him.

His allies had assured him they were still behind him after he'd told them of Dmitris' threat—as long as he delivered. *As long as he delivered.* It was also a threat, and they all knew it. They were growing impatient, but so was he. Hopefully, it was here in this ancient country that he'd finally find the answers he needed—starting with Elias and those pesky American federal agents.

~

Kalafat, Turkey
6:02 P.M.

As the explosion rattled their jail cell, smoke quickly filled it. Adrian closed her eyes and covered her mouth, coughing.

Above her, she heard keys jangle in the cell door and the amused chuckle of Myia, even as she coughed through the haze of smoke.

"Baris. Took you long enough," she said.

Adrian looked up. Baris, a short but powerfully built man, stood at the door of their cell. He gave Myia a twisted grin, revealing a row of yellowing teeth. He unlocked the cell door and reached into his backpack, handing them both guns and smoke masks.

"I arrive on time. Come now," he said in heavily accented English.

He turned to leave, with Adrian and Myia on his heels as they put on their masks. They hurried after him, racing down the smoke-filled corridor outside of their cell.

Footsteps pounded behind them, and they whirled. The officer who had locked them in their cell shouted something in Turkish, raising his weapon.

Baris fired at the officer, shouting at them to run. Adrian and Myia raced forward, soon reaching the back exit. Adrian looked around. There was no sign of Nick and Elias. She stopped.

"I'm not leaving without Nick!" she shouted.

"My friend has him and Elias—we have to go!" Myia hissed.

"No. Where is his cell?"

Myia glared, but she could see that Adrian wasn't budging. Myia turned and spoke to Baris in rapid Turkish as he approached.

"He with friend. We go now," he insisted.

From the other end of the corridor, she could hear the sounds of more footsteps and shouting. More police officers. Still, Adrian didn't budge.

"Where's his cell?" Adrian repeated.

"Back way we came to left," Baris replied.

"Adrian, if you get caught, you're on your own," Myia warned.

Adrian didn't hesitate. She turned, heading back the way they'd just come. Up ahead, she heard shouts and gunshots. She crouched into a protective stance, continuing forward, her weapon at the ready.

A hard male body slammed into her from behind. In the smoky haze of the corridor, it was difficult to tell who it was. She immediately went into attack mode, making her body go slack, whirling, raising her leg to knee him—

"Adrian!"

She looked up, stark relief filling her at the sight of Nick. Elias and another man, whom she assumed was Myia's other friend, were right behind him.

They turned, Nick taking her hand in his as they raced back down the corridor. They tore out of the back exit, ducking as several bullets ricocheted off the walls after them.

A run-down Toyota was waiting just outside

the exit, with Myia and Baris in the front seat. Myia leaned back to open the back doors for them as another officer scrambled out of the exit after them.

Adrian and Nick darted into the back seat, along with Elias. They ducked, bullets striking the car as Baris tore out of the parking lot.

CHAPTER 32

Izmir, Turkey
9:12 P.M.

Known as Smyrna in antiquity, the city of Izmir had roots dating back to prehistoric times. Its port was a key feature throughout its history and continued to be a source of economic importance to the modern city. Like many cities in the region, it had once been ruled by the Greeks, then the Romans, and finally the Ottomans. Now it was dotted with both skyscrapers from the current era, along with buildings and structures from various points in its past: tombs to old agoras from the Greco-Roman era, and bazaars from the time of the Ottomans.

Baris and Mehmet, Myia's friends, who'd freed them from the police station, had driven them into the city, taking them to a modest home in the Alsancak quarter, in the historic part of Izmir.

Once inside, Adrian and Nick immediately reached out to Briggs via a video call using Mehmet's encrypted laptop, informing him of their suspicious arrest by the local police.

"We barely escaped," Nick said. "We think we were tracked, possibly because of the flight we took from Heraklion, but we're not sure."

"Someone with influence bribed the local police to take us in. We can't trust law enforcement here. We don't know who to trust," Adrian added.

"I'll see what I can do about the police, but this is going to be a bureaucratic nightmare," Briggs said with a sigh of frustration. Briggs leaned toward the camera, lowering his voice. "Now, I'm not going to tell you to stay on the run and keep a low profile and find Atlantis before these dangerous people do. Officially, I'm going to tell you to find the nearest FBI office and await further instructions there."

Briggs met Adrian's eyes, and she grinned. This certainly wasn't the by-the-books Briggs who'd hunted her as a potential murder suspect during her time working the Cleopatra case.

"Officially, we'll take that into consideration," Nick replied with a straight face, though Adrian could hear the wink in his tone. "We'll reach out to you if we can. If we can't—"

"I understand," Briggs said, his expression turning serious. "We ran a full background on Lucas Dimou but weren't able to find anything suspicious, nothing criminal whatsoever. We're still looking into intel on criminal groups searching for a weapon with Atlantis, but so far, nothing. I'll keep doing what I can on my end."

"Thanks," Nick said. "Before you go, can we get confirmation that Elias' family is safe? And if possible, a safe contact number for his fiancée? He's worried about them, and I think it'll give him peace of mind."

"Sure," Briggs said. "Be careful, you two."

Adrian and Nick logged off the call. She looked at Nick, raising her eyebrows. "That was nice of you."

"You were right. The guy's just a scared curator whose back was up against the wall."

"Say that again?" Adrian teased.

"Ha ha. You were right. But . . . I see what you mean now. And I understand what it's like to do anything to protect someone that you love."

His gaze held hers for a moment, just a moment, before he got up to leave. Adrian watched him go, her pulse racing, before trailing him out to the living room, where Myia and Elias were seated with Baris and Mehmet.

During the drive to Izmir, Myia, speaking for Mehmet and Baris, since neither of them spoke much English, told Adrian and the others that they were brothers. They'd been friends with Myia for a decade; they were the ones who had introduced her to Socrates. Myia had told them of his murder but not much else for their own safety.

"Police here not our friends," Baris said, when Nick thanked them for taking the risk of helping them flee the police station, and by the dark look in his eyes, Adrian could tell there was a story there. Myia told them they'd used pressure bombs placed feet away from the exit and entrance of the small station, ensuring there was no one nearby to get injured. The whole point was to create a distraction, and it had worked.

"In case you're wondering," Myia added, giving Nick a long look, "Baris and Mehmet don't do what you think they do—and neither do I. We return artifacts to the home countries that Western museums have plundered. Museums from those countries pay us, off the record, to do so."

Nick said nothing, but surprise flickered across his features. Adrian studied Myia's defiant expression, seeing a different side to her. She'd initially just assumed Myia was a mercenary, but as their time together grew, she'd come to see Myia as fiercely loyal. Her suspicions that this was about more than money for her was proving to be correct. Myia hadn't asked about any type of reward since Heraklion, even after they'd gotten off their phone calls with Briggs.

"We talked to our boss. For now, we're on our own," Adrian informed Myia and Elias, as she and Nick stepped into the living room. "Going forward, we're going to have to be extra careful. But we still need to get to Miletus—without being detected this time."

Myia turned to Mehmet and Baris, speaking in

rapid Turkish. At their response, she beamed, giving the men a grateful nod.

"Baris is friends with a graduate student and archaeological assistant, Oran, who works at the site," she said. "There are excavations that are being carried out on an underground cave sanctuary. He can meet us at the site with records and tell us more about what's been uncovered there—and the site at large. He says there are back roads we can take, inaccessible to the public. But if we want to go undetected, it's best that we go at night, no tourists and no guards, which means we need to go now."

Miletus Archaeological Site
Balat, Aydin Province, Turkey
11:37 P.M.

THE RUINS of ancient Miletus were located two hours south of Izmir. Once surrounded by water, the site was now landlocked, with the ruins of buildings that told of its storied past dotting the landscape, from ancient Greek structures to buildings from the Byzantine era. At its height, Miletus had rivaled some of the greater Greek cities of the era, a center of trade and commerce, with a teeming population.

As they turned off the Izmir-Aydin highway, taking a back road that led to the rear of the site, where the current excavations were being carried out, Adrian could see the extensive ruins of Miletus in the distance, including the Greek-era grand theater. Mehmet parked on the side of the dirt road that cut into the rear of the site, taking out his binoculars to survey the excavation site from a distance. He paled, handing the binoculars to Myia.

Myia looked through them and let out a curse.

"What?" Adrian asked.

"See for yourself," Myia said with a sigh, handing her the binoculars.

Adrian took them and looked through the lenses, stiffening with dread. Two black SUVs were parked near the site, a group of men patrolling it, all armed to the teeth.

She stiffened with panic as a darkly handsome man and a tall, striking woman exited the excavation tent, the man dragging a younger Turkish man behind him and forcing him to his knees. A chill crept down Adrian's spine. This could be Oran, Baris' graduate school contact. The younger man looked up at him, pressing his hands together—he seemed to be pleading.

The man calmly took out a pistol and raised it, shooting the younger man point-blank. He slumped back onto the ground, his body going still.

CHAPTER 33

Horror filled Adrian's veins as the binoculars slipped from her hands. Nick took them from her and looked through the lenses, letting out a curse of his own.

In the distance, Adrian could see the SUVs racing away from the site. She stumbled back, hurrying toward the car. "They shot him!" she shouted. "We have to see if—"

She didn't have to finish her sentence. Mehmet had already started the car as they piled back in, and he raced toward the excavation site.

Once they reached it, Adrian and the others scrambled out of the car. Oran was on the ground, lying faceup, a gunshot wound to his chest, blood soaking the ground around him. Baris stumbled toward him, reaching for his pulse. He lowered his head and let out a cry of despair.

Adrian closed her eyes, guilt coursing through

her. This young man had only come here at this time of night to help them, and now he was dead.

But how did those men know he would be here?

Myia whirled toward Elias, obviously thinking the same thing, and for the first time since Heraklion, Adrian felt her own ripple of suspicion.

"I knew we shouldn't have trusted you!" Myia spat, glaring at Elias. "You're still working for those bastards, aren't you?"

Elias had been looking at the young man's body, his expression pale with shock. He looked up at Myia, stiffening with rage. He approached Myia, and in a quick move, took out her gun from her waistband.

Adrian started forward, but to her surprise, Elias handed Myia the gun, so that the barrel was pointed right at him.

"I was forced into this!" he spat, his eyes shimmering with tears. "I feel responsible for every single person hurt or killed by these men. So if you think that I'm willingly working for these monsters, *still*, then shoot me now."

The moment hung in the balance, rippling with tension. Adrian took a cautious step forward, her heart hammering.

"Myia, we're all upset. Let's just think logically."

Myia ignored Adrian, her focus on Elias, her hand wavering on the gun. Elias held her gaze, a torrent of emotions in his eyes.

Myia finally lowered her weapon, turning away from him. Elias' shoulders sank, but he still looked stricken, his eyes once again straying to the young man's body.

Adrian realized that Elias couldn't have reached out to anyone. He didn't have access to any phones or communication devices, and they'd been watching him like hawks since Heraklion. And he genuinely looked racked with guilt; no one was that good of an actor. She now felt guilty for her own stab of suspicion. Those men must have gotten to the site by reaching the same conclusion they did, especially if they knew about the labyrinth petroglyph in that cave on Crete.

"We need to call this in—and see what they took," she said.

They found nothing of note at the site; the man had either killed Oran because he wouldn't tell them anything, or they'd found whatever they needed. Regardless, Adrian knew they needed to find out what, if anything, they'd uncovered here.

As they drove back to Izmir, Nick placed a call to Vince on speaker.

"I thought you guys were supposed to be unofficially on the run," Vince answered, amusement in his tone. But the amusement faded when Adrian and Nick told him what happened.

"We need to get photos from that excavation site ASAP," Adrian said.

"I'll do what I can," Vince promised.

No one spoke much during the drive back to Izmir, the silence strained by shock, grief, and guilt.

Adrian thought about the man and woman she'd seen. The man had an air of authority, and the other men at the site—and the woman—had seemed to answer to him. Could he be Michalis and Lucas' employer? A head of this organization that Myia mentioned? Something told her he was. Yet when she described the man to Myia, she didn't recall him. She'd only remembered Michalis because of his scar.

When they returned to the house in Izmir, Myia turned to Adrian and the others. "We'll be right in. I want to talk to Baris and Mehmet alone for a minute."

Myia joined them moments later, followed by Baris and Mehmet, who headed to the closets, removing several bags.

"I told them they need to leave the country," Myia said quietly. "I can't live with more deaths on my conscience. It's bad enough that I dragged them into this. They pushed back, of course, but I told them they could be putting their families' lives in danger. That's the only way I could convince them to leave."

Adrian and Nick gave her an understanding nod. Myia approached Elias, who stiffened warily. She said something in a low tone to him, and he seemed to relax. He said nothing, but offered her a quick nod. Adrian wondered if their friendship would slowly but surely start to repair after their confrontation at Miletus.

After they'd seen Baris and Mehmet off, thanking them profusely for their help, they made their way to the guest bedrooms that Myia had pointed out. Elias bid them good night and entered his room, while Nick lingered as Adrian stopped in front of hers.

"You've been quiet since we left the site," he said. "You OK?"

"No," she said honestly. "That kid—Oran? He was just trying to help us."

"That wasn't your fault," Nick insisted. "There's nothing more you could have done. Trust me, we all feel guilty. But I know how long you can carry guilt, and how much it weighs on you."

Adrian knew what he was referring to—the case of the missing college student who had turned up dead before she could solve it, during her initial stint at the bureau. That case had filled her with so much frustration and guilt, she'd left the bureau and law enforcement altogether before getting drawn back in. Nick was right; she did have a habit of feeling every unsolved case, her innate need to right wrongs. She wondered if it all went back to the loss of her father . . . her constant need to fill an emptiness that was impossible to do so.

"I'll try," she whispered.

Nick reached up to touch her cheek, his hand lingering there. Adrian had to stop herself from leaning into his touch. After a moment that was all too brief, Nick dropped his hand and stepped away, muttering a quick good night before disappearing into his room.

7:02 A.M.

Adrian's vibrating phone woke her from her restless sleep. She blinked, rubbing her eyes. She still felt groggy; she'd tossed and turned for most of the night, wondering about those men and what they could have found, the identity of the man she suspected was the leader of this mysterious organization, and plagued with lingering guilt over the death of Baris' friend, Oran.

She sat up, picking up her phone and looking at the screen. There was a text message from Vince, sent to both her and Nick.

> You're really going to want to check your email. Like . . . really.

Moments later, Adrian and the others were crowded around a laptop that Baris had loaned to Myia before he left. Nick opened his email, clicking on a link. Two dozen photos instantly downloaded onto the screen.

"Vince does it again," Nick said, shaking his head in amazement.

The photos were taken from the excavation site. There were various photos of artifacts taken from the underground cave sanctuary: libation vessels, clay shards, votive offerings.

But her focus was centered on several photos in particular. They were all of a labyrinth petroglyph, carved into the wall, a near replica to the one they'd found in the cave on Crete.

And just like the one in Crete, there was writing in the center, but this writing was Cretan hieroglyphs, an even older undeciphered script than Linear A. Yet she had the gut feeling the writing stated the same thing as the petroglyph in Crete. Atai. Atlantis.

CHAPTER 34

Izmir, Turkey
7:15 A.M.

They all stared at the photographs on the screen in amazement for several moments, until Adrian broke the silence.

"OK. We have another labyrinth petroglyph along with what I assume is the word Atlantis, from a time even earlier than the peak sanctuary in Crete," Adrian said. "What's the significance?"

"It's likely akin to what we found in Crete—a prayer, a longing to return to their original home," Elias said.

"This could explain why the Minoans chose to go there. Maybe it was an original home of theirs, and their ancestors also had a memory of Atlantis—going further back in time," Adrian mused.

"What if it's also pointing toward the actual Atlantis?" Nick offered. "I think we can argue that the further we go back in time, the closer we'll get to a historical Atlantis."

Adrian nodded her agreement. She turned to Elias. "Can you look into your database for other petroglyphs of the labyrinth in the Mediterranean region? I know there are many, but maybe we can narrow it down to ones that date even further back in time than this one."

"It looks like there's one that predates this petroglyph in Sardinia," Elias said, several moments later, after he'd logged in and performed a search. "And it looks pretty similar to the one in Miletus—and Crete."

He turned the screen to face them, revealing the faint image of a labyrinth carved into the wall of a tomb. It wasn't as large as the labyrinth they'd found in the peak sanctuary cave in Crete, nor did it have any writing, but the design was eerily similar.

"This petroglyph is in the Luzzanas rock tomb, or the 'Tomba de Labrinto,'" Elias continued. "Now, to be fair, the exact dating of it is uncertain, but it's commonly assumed to be as early as 2500 BC. The tomb consists of at least four, possibly more, chambers that are interconnected and haven't been fully excavated. It's one of dozens of 'Domus de Janas'—prehistoric underground tombs all throughout Sardinia."

Adrian studied the image of the labyrinth, thinking of what she knew about Sardinia's ancient history. It was dominated by a Bronze Age society known as the Nuragic civilization, named for the *nuraghe* structures they built—megalithic towers, the ruins of many still dotted the island of Sardinia to this day. The nuraghe and their builders had fascinated even the ancient Greeks, who came up with legends to describe how they'd built such grand structures. It was considered an advanced society by even the ancients.

"Do you think the Bronze Age Sardinians—the Nuragic civilization—could have a connection with a historical Atlantis?" she asked Elias.

"Like many ancient Mediterranean civilizations—as we've seen with Troy, for example—there have been those who have assumed that Sardinia was Atlantis itself, with its Nuragic civilization and impressive yet mysterious megalithic buildings, along with its important strategic position in the Mediterranean. But I don't think it's Atlantis. There is something else, though. The Bronze Age collapse connection. Remember how I mentioned the mysterious Sea Peoples who invaded Egypt and other civilizations during the collapse? One of them, the Sherden, is commonly believed to have been the ancient Sardinians."

Adrian imagined the native Sardinians, like the Minoans, watching their society collapse around them, invading other lands as their own were depleted of resources. She wondered if they had also inscribed the labyrinth symbol onto the wall of this tomb as a prayer, a beseeching to the gods to help them return to their original home.

She thought of the writing in the cave in Crete, and on this petroglyph, written in undeciphered scripts in uncertain languages, though many linguists assumed the scripts were of the Minoan language, a pre-Greek language. Her mind seized on the notion of the pre-Greek languages, another thought occurring to her.

"The pre-Greek languages," she said slowly. "That could be another connection. No one knows for sure what language the Sardinians of the Bronze Age spoke, though theories abound, from Proto-Iberian to Ligurian. There is one theory that states they spoke a pre-Indo-European language, as many theorize that Minoan was."

She considered the ancient word for Atlantis in pre-Greek. Atai. Could the ancient Sardinians have had a similar language to the Minoans because they ultimately had a shared origin?

"So you're saying . . . " Myia said slowly.

"That these pre-Greek, pre-Indo-European languages may have had a shared origin, going all the way back to Atlantis," Adrian said. "They were spoken in prehistoric times, long before even Proto-Greek. They're not connected to Indo-European, and there are theories as to what language family they could belong to. I would have considered this theory insane before the discovery of Solon's papyrus, but I think there may be something to it." As a linguist, excitement rippled through Adrian at the thought of uncovering the mystery of pre-Greek languages, and their connection to an even older society, Atlantis.

"I think we have enough to know where we need to go next," Nick said.

~

Athens, Greece
11:08 A.M.

ATHENA FOLLOWED TOBIAS' car as it wove through the heavy traffic of central Athens. She'd followed him yesterday from CHSR's offices, but he'd only gone to police headquarters from there, staying until late evening before going to his home in the Pangrati neighborhood.

Athena had remained parked all night, several houses away from his home, fighting to stay awake, not wanting to risk losing him if he left. She'd had the foresight to bring a change of clothes and her toothbrush for her stakeout adventure, but knew she'd have to shower; she was just terrified of losing him. He was connected to all of this, and if she could just figure out how, it would bring her closer to figuring out who had killed her partner and why.

As she followed him now, it looked like he wasn't heading to police headquarters. He was taking a different route. If he was heading back to CHSR, maybe she could follow him in. She still wore her disguise.

He turned onto Katechaki Avenue, one of the

main roads of Athens that led outside of the city. Athena stayed two cars back, keeping her gaze trained on his black Audi. He made a sudden abrupt turn off Katechaki, and Athena almost lost him. She quickly made the turn as well.

They were now in the suburb of Neo Psychiko, and he maneuvered his car through the narrow streets, Athena following close behind, until he made another abrupt turn.

Athena trailed, her blood turning to ice when she realized he'd turned into an alley with a dead end.

He'd spotted her.

Tobias slammed on his brakes, stopping in the middle of the alley. Her heart in her throat, Athena started to back up, but another car pulled in behind her in the alley, blocking her in.

Athena scrambled for her service weapon, but Tobias was fast, arriving at her window with his own weapon leveled at her head.

"Lieutenant Constable Karras," he said, giving her a regrettable shake of his head. "It seems you're just as foolish as your dead partner."

CHAPTER 35

Sassari Province, Sardinia
8:46 P.M.

Illuminated only by moonlight, Adrian could make out the lushly verdant landscape of the Sardinian countryside, from rolling green hills and sprawling farmland to quaint villages. Given its extensive history, from its earliest inhabitants during the Paleolithic era to the indigenous Nuragic civilization, the landscape evoked a place locked in time, unaffected by the modern era. It would be fitting, Adrian thought, if they could find the key to locating the ultimate ancient civilization here.

They had flown in from the international airport in Izmir to Alghero Airport in Sardinia with the task force's help, using fake passports now that the police in Turkey were after them. Now they were making their way west through the countryside toward Benetutti, the closest town to the Luzzanas tomb, in their rental.

Neither Elias nor Myia had any contacts in the country, so they were completely on their own. They'd decided to head to the site at night to avoid any tourists who might be in the area.

As they had in Miletus, Nick parked the car roughly a mile away from the site once they got close. The tomb was difficult to spot from this distance, as it was in the center of a flat field with nothing distinctive to mark its location; they were relying on both physical maps they'd bought at the airport and the maps on their phones.

Adrian took out the binoculars, angry frustration filling her at the sight of a lone car parked there. Unless there just happened to be some tourist who wanted to see the tomb at night, someone had beat them to it—possibly men from this organization.

"What are we going to do?" Myia asked, heaving a sigh after she and Nick had looked through the binoculars as well.

"We could play it safe and stay out of sight until these people—whoever they are—leave," Adrian said. "Or..."

"Or?" Nick pressed.

"We can take them on. There's only one car; there can't be many of them. If they are tourists, we can scare them away with our badges. If not... we have the element of surprise. We can't risk them being one step ahead of us."

"I agree," Nick said. "Besides," he added with a wink, "the safe option is always the boring one."

Moments later, Adrian and Nick moved through the field adjacent to the creek bed that led to the tomb, crouched low, their weapons clutched in their hands. Myia was trailing twenty feet behind as additional backup. Elias had remained with the car, watching them with the binoculars, ready to serve as their getaway driver if it came down to it.

They'd come a long way with trust since the confrontation at Miletus. Adrian had half expected Nick or Myia to protest leaving Elias behind. Instead, they'd just nodded their agreement when she suggested it.

Adrian and Nick continued to creep toward the opening of the tomb. No one had emerged, and the car was still parked next to it; she only prayed there weren't many of them, or at the very least, they were tourists.

There was only the sound of Adrian's pounding heart and her breathing as they got closer. She was glad, as always, that Nick was at her side. He moved cautiously yet with confidence, his body alert as they made their way forward.

They stopped when they were a dozen feet

away from the opening of the tomb, which was merely a carved-out hole in the ground. She listened, hearing the rumble of two male voices beneath them. Two men. Relief rushed through Adrian—they had a shot.

She looked at Nick, holding up her hand and counting down to three before they charged forward, descending into the tomb, turning on the flashlights they held with their service weapons to guide their way.

Even filled with rocks and featuring low ceilings, the tomb was surprisingly spacious and wide open. There were several square openings carved into the walls where once remains and treasures had lain, but were now filled with crumbling rocks. On the left wall she could see the labyrinth petroglyph inscribed.

But her attention immediately went to the two men who were inside, shining their flashlights around in the darkness. The men whirled to face them, an older man in his fifties and a younger one in his twenties. The younger man immediately reached to his holster for his weapon.

"Hold it!" Nick shouted. "Keep still. Hands where I can see them. I *will* shoot."

The younger man glowered, looking as if he were going to defy him, but the older man reached out, placing a placating hand on his arm. He kept his other arm raised to indicate he was unarmed.

"Zacharias, it's OK," he said. He turned his focus to Adrian. "Are you Adrian West?"

Adrian blinked in surprise, but remained on guard, keeping her weapon trained on him.

"Who's asking?" she demanded.

"Dmitris Karagiannis. I want to help you stop a dangerous man from finding Atlantis."

CHAPTER 36

As Adrian and Nick stared at Dmitris in disbelief, Myia stepped forward, shaking with fury, her gun still leveled at his chest.

"Why should we believe you?" she snarled.

Zacharias' hand strayed to his weapon, but Dmitris stopped him.

"Because if Stephanos succeeds, it will be the end of us all. And I want to stop that."

Dmitris turned to Zacharias, giving him a nod. Zacharias hesitated, his gaze sliding from Myia's hostile expression to Adrian and Nick, who were watching him cautiously. He seemed to come to an internal decision, removing his gun and tossing it to the ground.

"This is my son, Zacharias. I understand why you would be wary of trusting us. Hear me out, and let me prove it to you."

9:22 P.M.

Adrian stood opposite Dmitris and Zacharias, reeling from all that he'd told them: everything about CHSR, the modern iteration of an ancient secret society, Stephanos Keliades' plans for worldwide destruction to restart civilization anew, and the weapon of Greek fire he sought at the site to help further his plans.

She and the others had been spot-on with their assumption about this organization's intentions for Atlantis. A part of her had hoped she was wrong, that they just sought it for the treasures it held for profit, though Dmitris told her that was a goal as well.

Adrian and the others were gathered around their rental and Dmitris' car, now parked farther away from the site, though they were still close enough to it to see if anyone else approached.

"I grew up with Stephanos' father, Alexandrios," Dmitris continued, his expression shadowing with grief. "Both of our fathers had long been members, and their fathers before them. At first, I was proud to be part of such an organization with such an ancient history, until I learned what some members were intent on doing—including Alexandros. He was obsessed with the Bronze Age collapse. He was convinced we needed something similar to happen in modern times. I confronted him, but he was steadfast in his beliefs. I thought I could convince him otherwise, and when he became ill with cancer, I'd hoped his priorities had shifted. But I learned soon after he died that his son had taken on his plans. Alexandros heavily indoctrinated his son in his beliefs. I taught my own son differently, that humanity is inherently good and worth fighting for," he added, his gaze sliding to Zacharias. Zacharias, who was silent but listening intently, gave his father a small smile and nod of confirmation.

"The other leaders aren't thrilled with Stephanos. They think he's too impulsive, and those who know of his plans are either fully aligned with him, or don't take him seriously and aren't doing anything to stop him," Dmitris continued. "They're more concerned with the treasures that Atlantis will bring forth. I've been pretending to go along with Stephanos' plans, even with him taking the papyrus, though I intended to turn him in before he ever got to Atlantis. I've been doing my own parallel investigation ever since the papyrus was discovered."

"Why did he steal the papyrus?" Nick asked.

"There are long-held rumors in our organization that there's some sort of map hidden on it, a map that leads to Atlantis. That rumor turned out to not be true, as he obviously hasn't found it," Dmitris replied.

Adrian stiffened, a thought occurring to her. "Were you the one who sent men to Elias at the hospital?"

Dmitris looked regretful. "I did. I learned that

Stephanos had one of his men approach Elias, and I wanted to see what he knew. They were ordered not to harm anyone; the guns were just supposed to be a show of force. I was angered when I learned they'd injured that police constable. But I had to move quickly. I was afraid Stephanos would send his men to eliminate Elias after the theft. I couldn't risk it."

"What about Socrates—Ben Grant?" Myia demanded. "Were you behind what happened to him as well?"

"Socrates?" Dmitris echoed with a confused frown. He swore, closing his eyes. "I underestimated how murderous Stephanos has become. And no, to answer your question, I had nothing to do with that. I'm trying to save lives, not eliminate them."

Adrian studied Dmitris, considering everything he'd told them. Ever since Elias' betrayal, she'd second-guessed her instincts, the ones that were now telling her to trust him. But . . . she had been right about Elias deep down. He'd been forced to help Michalis and had become a useful ally. And she'd been right about the intent of the organization behind all this.

"I understand if you don't trust me, but we don't have much time. Stephanos' team of experts are probably on the way here as well. We're at a dead end here; we found nothing in the tomb other than the petroglyph. We've sent it to a trusted expert friend of mine—someone who has nothing to do with CHSR—and he hasn't been able to tell me much. When you found us, we were trying to see if there was anything else of note in the tomb, but we found nothing," Dmitris said.

"Give me one second," Adrian said. She turned to Nick, Myia, and Elias, and they stepped away from Dmitris and Zacharias. "What do we think?"

"I think he's telling the truth. He has resources, and he's a member of this organization, so he has useful information. I think we can make significant progress if we work together," Nick said.

"You know me—I don't trust anyone," Myia muttered. "But Nick has a point. We're at another dead end, and we need all the help we can get, as you keep saying, Adrian. That being said, if he even blinks wrong, I'm killing him myself," she added, her tone quiet but ferocious.

When Adrian looked at Elias, he gave her a rueful grin. "I'm all about trusting people. It's the only reason I'm standing here now."

Adrian moved back over to Dmitris, her mind made up. "You're right. There isn't much time. We need to get to Atlantis before Stephanos." She glanced back in the tomb's direction, her mind racing. "What if we've been too focused on the labyrinth petroglyphs?" she asked. "Yes, the symbol is very important and could likely point to Atlantis, but we believe—"

"The Atlanteans spread out over the isles of the Mediterranean over time?" Dmitris interrupted. At her nod, he continued. "That's the same thing the ancient members of our society believed. They just couldn't pinpoint the location of their origin."

She turned to Elias. "Can you think of anything else here in Sardinia that would link to other places we've been? Something besides the labyrinth symbol—maybe similar to the peak sanctuaries in Crete?"

"You have to consider geography," Elias said. "Crete is mountainous, so there are many peak and cave sanctuaries. Here on Sardinia, the ancients favored megalithic structures, such as nuraghes, which could have served a variety of purposes. There are also holy wells, which were built to worship water. Like the peak sanctuaries in Crete, both nuraghes and holy wells are all over the island."

"Is there a holy well or nuraghe nearby? A significant one that was built around the time of the collapse?" Nick asked.

"There is a major one not too far from here—the well of Santa Cristina," Elias replied.

CHAPTER 37

Paulilatino, Sardinia
10:58 P.M.

The well temple was located at the sanctuary of Santa Cristina, near the town of Paulilatino. It derived its name from the church of Santa Cristina built in the eleventh century, adjacent to the temple.

It was located an hour's drive south of the tomb, closer to Sardinia's eastern coast. Again, they stopped a distance away, scanning the site with their binoculars to make certain no one was there before they drew closer. They still parked a half mile away in case they needed to make a quick escape without being detected.

As they approached the temple, Adrian could make out the greater extent of the site, even in the dark. It included the well temple, a nuraghe, the medieval church, and homes for pilgrims that were still used to this day.

Once they got close to the exterior of the well temple, Adrian let out a low gasp of awe. It was one thing for Elias to describe it, but to see it in person was simply breathtaking.

The well temple was set in a *temenos,* a sacred enclosure, built in the shape of a lock. From her vantage point, she could see the triangular staircase that descended downward toward the well, giving the effect of a reverse staircase as one descended. She stopped to take it in for a moment; the temple looked sacred in the moonlight. She could imagine the ancient Sardinians' reverence as they came here to worship.

Zacharias remained outside the temple as a lookout as Adrian and the others entered and descended the staircase, using flashlights to guide their way. The steps led to a subterranean room, where an opening in the ceiling allowed moonlight to spill in. The pool at the bottom was a still active spring that Elias told them the Sardinians had purposefully built this temple around.

"It's something, isn't it?" Elias said. "There are theories that in additional to a temple, it was an astronomical observatory. The sun shines directly into the staircase leading down into the well during the equinoxes."

Adrian took in the sharp geometric shapes of the temple, which suggested harmony. Everything in the temple seemed purposeful in design. Her thoughts turned to the peak sanctuaries on Crete, and her theory that they'd served as directional waypoints.

"Which direction does the temple face?" she asked Elias.

"I believe it faces east," he replied.

"If the peak sanctuaries on Crete were directional way points, what if the well temples—or the nuraghes—were as well?" she asked.

Dmitris stepped forward, taking a tablet out of his bag. "We've already plotted out the nuraghes and well temples all over the island. My expert also suspected they were important."

He tapped a button on the tablet and handed it to her. Adrian studied it; on the screen was a map of the island with digital dots that indicated the well temples and nuraghes.

Nick, Myia, and Elias stepped forward, looking over her shoulder at the map. At first glance, they appeared scattered haphazardly all over the island, but as Adrian studied the general direction the well temples faced . . . they all appeared to point east.

"Elias, what's east of here?" she asked, her heart hammering.

Before Elias could respond, Zacharias raced down the stairs, his face white with panic.

"There are about a half-dozen SUVs in the distance—coming this way," he said. "We have to get out of here. *Now.*"

CHAPTER 38

At Zacharias' words, Adrian stiffened with dread. Dmitris stepped forward, his expression urgent.

"Get them to the airport—make sure the plane is ready. Tell the pilot to fly east until you've nailed down a location. If it's Stephanos, I'll do my best to buy you some time."

Zacharias froze, his face going pale. "Dad, I don't—"

"That's an order, son. You know this is bigger than you or me." He turned to the others. "Go. When I can, I'll be in touch."

They obliged, racing up the stairs and back out of the temple. Behind them, she heard the deep rumble of Dmitris' voice as he murmured something that sounded reassuring to Zacharias before he hurried out after them.

They darted away from the temple and toward their rental, leaving Dmitris' car behind with him.

Adrian chanced a glance backward; in the distance she could see a line of SUVs approaching. Dmitris watched them go for a moment, his body tense, before he turned to face the approaching vehicles.

Adrian picked up her pace, and they soon reached their rental. Nick took the wheel, and they sped away from the site, keeping their headlights off to avoid being detected.

She turned to look out the back window as Nick drove away. She could see the SUVs pulling to a stop at the site, one by one. In the back seat, Zacharias was pale, continually turning to look out the back window. He closed his eyes as if to pull himself together before taking out his phone and sending a text.

"I just texted our pilot. The sooner you guys can come up with a location, the better."

Adrian turned to Elias, who was seated between Myia and Zacharias in the backseat.

"What's significant to Sardinia—to Atlantis—that's east of here?" she asked.

"There's Spain, of course, but there's also the Balearic Islands," Elias replied after a brief pause.

"The Balearic Islands—as in the party island of Ibiza?" Nick asked. He'd turned the headlights back on once they were out of sight of the temple, but had increased his speed. Though his tone was light and playful, his grip on the steering wheel was tight, his knuckles white as his gaze repeatedly went to the rearview mirror.

"They are far more than party islands. They

have a rich and varied history," Elias returned with a scowl. "In the prehistoric period—"

"Give us a history lesson later. We need to know if this is linked. We don't know how long Dmitris can hold off those men," Myia interrupted.

"There have been labyrinth petroglyphs found on several sites around the Balearic Islands. There was even a tribe called the Balares tribe in ancient Sardinia. They're believed to have come directly from the Balearics, hence their name. There are also similar buildings on the Balearic Islands to the ones found in Sardinia, megalithic buildings called 'talaiots,' akin to nuraghes in Sardinia."

Adrian turned to face Nick and Myia. Elias' words were convincing enough for her. She had the gut instinct that they were getting closer.

"Patrick," Zacharias said, again taking out his phone and placing the call on speaker. "I have a destination for you. Take us to Palma Airport on Mallorca in the Balearic Islands."

11:27 P.M.

Fury coursed through Stephanos as he emerged from his SUV to find Dmitris standing near the well temple of Santa Cristina. He itched to take out his pistol and execute him, just as he had that useless archaeologist assistant back in Miletus, but he had the feeling that wouldn't be as satisfying.

He'd been in a foul mood once they'd reached the site of Miletus, having learned that Elias and his American friends had escaped from the jail. They'd evaded him—again. It was a pleasant surprise to find someone at the Miletus site, where his experts had recommended they explore due to its connections with the Minoans. But the kid hadn't given him any useful information, mainly, what he was doing there at that time of night. He should have taken the time to torture the answers out of him, but he didn't have the patience.

The kid had brought photos of the excavations at Miletus, and those photos had led them to Sardinia. He, Irina, and his men had been here all day, stopping at several spots around the island that his experts deemed relevant, yet nothing significant had materialized so far, and he was growing more and more frustrated.

Dmitris approached him with his customary imperious look, and Stephanos quelled his fury. He would let the older man hang himself with his own rope before executing him.

"What are you doing here?" Stephanos asked tightly.

"I was getting tired of you dragging your feet," Dmitris snapped. "I had an expert of my own tell me about this place."

Stephanos glared. The nerve of this asshole. "So you came out here all on your own?"

"I'm allowed to take things into my own hands

when I feel they aren't being handled properly," Dmitris said coldly.

Stephanos stared at him for a long moment before looking around. "Where's your shadow—or should I say, your little boy? He doesn't breathe unless you tell him to."

"Some things are better handled alone," Dmitris said, but Stephanos noticed he'd paled when he mentioned his son.

"I'm done with this game," Stephanos said with an impatient sigh, taking out his pistol. "You know that I know what you're up to, but I'll give you points for attempting a cover story, even if it is a stupid one."

He leveled his pistol at Dmitris' head, relishing in the look of fear that played across the older man's features. He wasn't so imperious now.

"Your father," Dmitris spat, "would be ashamed of the man you've become."

Stephanos' fury flared to life. He slammed the butt of the pistol into Dmitris' temple, continuing to hit him even after he went down, over and over, until Dmitris' blood splattered onto his face and shirt.

It was Irina who stopped him.

"Not yet, Stephanos. We need to find out what he knows. And you have leverage over him. His son. You can execute him after we find Atlantis."

Stephanos stepped back, his chest heaving, allowing his fury to recede. Dmitris was lying in a crumpled heap on the ground in front of him, his face a bloody mess, struggling to breathe. Stephanos ached to finish the job, to beat the man to death, his words about his father echoing in his mind. But Irina was right.

"My father would be proud of me, and ashamed of you. I made him a promise on his deathbed that I've dedicated my life to fulfill—and I will fulfill it. You're the coward who doesn't have the courage to do what needs to be done."

He straightened and gestured to two of his men. "Put him in the back. He's coming with us."

CHAPTER 39

Airspace over the Balearic Sea
2:37 A.M.

Adrian looked out the window of the private plane, down at the dark waters of the Balearic. Under different circumstances, she could imagine traveling to a tourist destination on one of the islands that made up the Balearic Island chain. But the situation was far from idyllic. Even now, adrenaline pumped through her veins as she thought of what lay ahead of them.

They had arrived at Alghero Airport to find Dmitris' private plane ready to go and waiting for them on the tarmac. They'd barely buckled their seatbelts before they were ascending.

"Are you sure the Balearic Islands are where we should go?" Zacharias had asked Elias, as the plane reached maximum altitude.

"No," Elias said bluntly, "but what we saw in Sardinia seems to point in their direction."

"What do we know about the natives who inhabited them?" Adrian asked.

"The Balearics have been populated since around 2500 to 2300 BC, with the population migrating from southern France or the Iberian Peninsula. Not too much is known about those early peoples; much of what we do know is from Greco-Roman writers. The natives, at first, lived in caves and rock formations. They were the ones to construct megalithic buildings called the talaiots, akin to the nuraghes in Sardinia. The talaiots served many functions—they were funerary, territorial markers, ceremonial centers, watchtowers, or religious sanctuaries for rituals. There are hundreds spread around Mallorca, the largest island of the Balearics, alone."

Elias told them about the necropolises that existed on the islands as well, but they decided to focus on talaiots, as they seemed to serve the same purpose as the peak sanctuaries in Crete and the well temples and nuraghes in Sardinia. Using topographic surveys that Zacharias provided, and archaeological records that Elias was able to access, they decided to start with several Talaiotic sites on Mallorca. Two were well preserved while one hadn't been as heavily excavated as the others. They had to move fast. She knew there wasn't much time; Stephanos could be right on their heels—if he wasn't already there.

Adrian turned her focus from the window to Myia and Elias, who were seated across the aisle from her. They were in deep conversation, and she even caught them smiling a couple of times. Zacharias sat alone in the front of the plane, continually checking his phone, his body tense; she knew he was worried about his father. She'd thanked him for his help and told him they'd do whatever they could to help his father if he was in danger; he'd only offered grunts in response. She'd decided to leave him alone and give him space.

"Think we're going to the right place?" Nick asked, taking the seat next to her.

"I hope so. If not, we're soon going to run out of Mediterranean islands," she said, giving him a wry smile.

Nick chuckled, leaning back in his seat. "If the fate of the world wasn't at stake, I could almost pretend we were traveling for vacation."

"I was thinking the same thing."

Nick studied her for a long moment. "Once we're done saving the world—and I hope we succeed—what do you say—"

The pilot announcing their initial descent into Palma interrupted him. Nick blinked, as if the pilot's voice had brought him back to reality. He stiffened, giving her an awkward smile as he got up to return to his seat.

As they buckled up for their descent, Myia turned to give her a knowing look. Had she overheard Nick? Adrian avoided her gaze, turning to look out of the window, forcing herself to prepare for what lay ahead . . . and not wonder what Nick had been about to say.

~

Unknown
2:45 A.M.

ATHENA WRAPPED her arms around herself, shivering in the dank cold of the cellar.

Tobias had dragged her from her car and jabbed her in the neck with something that knocked her out. She'd come to, here, her wig removed, her head throbbing.

She wasn't sure where she was, but she suspected she was still in Athens; in the distance, she could rear the rumble of traffic. She'd tried screaming and banging against the door, but silence was her only response. She also wasn't certain how long she'd been here, but her stomach was growling with hunger. Had Tobias brought her here to starve to death and waste away? Terror filled her at the thought, and she closed her eyes, taking a shuddering breath.

She jumped at the sound of grinding; someone was pushing open the cellar door. Tobias entered, shutting the door behind him and leaning against it, clutching a gun in his hand. Panic surged in her belly, but she quelled it. If she was going to survive, this was her chance.

Tobias sneered down at her, and she realized he was taking dark pleasure in her predicament. *Get him talking*, she told herself. *And keep him talking.*

"CHSR . . . they're behind all of this, aren't they? The papyrus theft, Stavros' death?"

"CHSR is so much more than what you think. Like most people, you're blind to what's in front of you," he snapped.

"What am I blind to?"

Tobias studied her for a moment before chuckling. "I see what you're doing, Karras. You forget that I'm a cop too. Keep him talking, right? But I'll indulge you," he said, shaking his head. "CHSR goes back for millennia, and it's preserved the ancient wisdom. Destruction is the way to renewal, and only destruction."

"What do you mean?" Athena asked, terror cascading down her spine.

"There are those who doubt Stephanos, but he's as great as his father was. He will bring the end we need. I believe in him, even though others don't," Tobias muttered, ignoring her question, his gaze focused on the wall behind her head. His eyes now glittered with madness. "The end is the only way to get to the beginning."

"The end of what?" Athena pressed.

Tobias looked at her as if remembering she was there, and a cruel smile curled his lips. "I've indulged you enough. It's a tragedy what happened to Athena Karras," he said. "Distraught over the suicide of her partner, she took her own life as well.

A shame. She had such a promising career ahead of her."

For such a tall man, he moved fast. Tobias lunged toward her, yanking her up off the ground by her shirt and slamming her against the wall. Pain radiated throughout her body, and she was weak with fatigue and hunger, but she used all her strength to lift her knee—

He tsked at her and shifted his body, evading her attempted attack. His gun was out now, pressed beneath her chin, his eyes wild.

"Your partner fought as well. But he couldn't stop this. No one can."

As he started to pull the trigger, Yiannis charged into the cellar with two other officers. The officers tackled Tobias to the ground, wrestling his gun away from him as Yiannis rushed over to Athena.

"Athena," Yiannis said, his eyes scanning over her form with worry. "Gavril tracked Tobias' phone after you went missing. Are you OK?"

Stark relief filled Athena, and tears filled her eyes. She couldn't believe how close she'd come to death.

"I've been investigating Tobias as well. I'm sorry I couldn't tell you. I had to be very careful with who knew. I had to pretend to go along with the official story of Stavros' suicide."

Athena nodded, still reeling, but made herself focus. "Tobias gave me a name—Stephanos. We have to stop him."

CHAPTER 40

Port de Pollenca, Mallorca
11:14 A.M.

Adrian made her way up the hill that led to the ruins of the ancient city of Bocchoris, trailing Zacharias, Myia, and Elias. Nick brought up the rear, and by the look on his face, she could tell that he was feeling just as defeated as she was.

After arriving in the bustling capital city of Palma late last night, they'd driven to Mallorca's north coast, where they'd spent the night at a modern three-story villa perched on the cliffs overlooking the bay of Pollenca. Zacharias told them the villa belonged to one of Dmitris' ex-mistresses whom he was still friendly with and who was currently out of the country.

They'd left the villa early that morning. Bocchoris was the last of the sites they'd visited: the other two, a well-reserved Talaiotic village near the tourist town of S'illot, on the east coast of the island, and another site near Son Oleza, also on the island's east coast, while displaying impressive ruins of ancient buildings, had turned up nothing of use. Her anxiety had grown with each stop, and she was starting to fear they were in the wrong place.

Bocchoris was near the town of Port de Pollenca, where the ruins were elevated on a small hill. It dated back to 1400 BCE and had eventually become a federated city of the Roman Empire before falling into ruin centuries later. It was difficult to find, as not much of the ancient city remained other than some crumbling walls, gateposts, and the remains of a talaiot, along with the fragments of a naveta, an ancient chamber tomb. Rocks, tall grasses, and overgrown shrubs covered the entire site; they had to navigate carefully to not lose their balance on the uneven ground.

Zacharias' topographic surveys of the area confirmed there was an extensive narrow tunnel beneath the ruins of the talaiot here. If it weren't for the survey, Adrian would have skipped the site altogether, given the fragmentary state of the ruins.

They finally reached the ruins of the talaiot, which was distinguished only by a row of ancient stones. Working together, they pushed aside the grasses that surrounded the ruins, and with great effort, they move aside several of the crumbling stones at the base, revealing a narrow opening beneath.

Adrian dropped down onto her haunches, shining her flashlight into the opening. What she saw corroborated with the survey. The tunnel seemed to burrow deep into the side of the hill.

"I'm going in," Adrian said, straightening and dropping her backpack. She took out her headlamp and strapped it on.

"I'm coming with you," Nick said immediately.

"Nick—" Adrian began, eyeing the small crawlspace.

"I'm coming with you," he repeated, his tone firm, and she knew there was no arguing with him.

Moments later, they both were on their bellies, crawling into the tunnel beneath the talaiot. It was pitch black. Even the light on their headlamps created little illumination. The tunnel gradually descended, growing larger, and she and Nick were eventually able to stand, though they had to crouch low—especially Nick with his tall frame.

Adrian took out her flashlight to create even more illumination, scanning around as they cautiously moved forward. Yet so far, she was only seeing darkness, the dirt walls around her and the dusty ground below.

She froze when speckles of dirt from the ceiling fell around them. Fear filled her; she didn't know how stable this tunnel was or the likelihood of it caving in around them.

Her frustration growing, she shined her flashlight around, uncertain if it was safe for them to keep going.

"Adrian," Nick said abruptly. He was looking past her, his eyes wide. "Behind you. On the ground."

She followed Nick's gaze. Roughly six feet behind her, scrawled into the ground, were faint petroglyphs. *Multiple* petroglyphs.

Adrian and Nick ventured forward, shining their lights on the petroglyphs. Her heart picked up its pace as she brushed away the dirt that covered them. The petroglyphs were labyrinths—or at least early forms of them—with not as many circular pathways as the ones they'd found in Crete and Miletus. There were twelve of them arranged on the ground. In two of them, bulls were drawn in the center.

"Oh my God," Adrian whispered in awe. She straightened, taking out her phone and snapping multiple photos of the petroglyphs. As she did so, more dirt fell down around them.

Adrian stilled. Up ahead, dirt continued to fall from the ceiling, and she realized it was happening—the tunnel was caving in on them.

CHAPTER 41

Nick and Adrian tore back down the tunnel as dirt continued to spill around them. They reached the part of the tunnel that ascended into a narrow crawlspace and hurried inside, moving as fast as they could on a crawl. The tunnel behind them was beginning to fully cave in—if they didn't get to the opening fast enough, they'd be trapped.

Adrian moved as fast as she could, panic clogging her veins, her pulse racing. Every movement she made seemed agonizingly slow. The tunnel was rapidly deteriorating all around them, and it was only a matter of seconds before there would be no way out. That feeling of claustrophobia tugged on her senses at the thought of being buried alive. She forced herself to move even faster, until she saw the shaft of light at the end of the tunnel.

She scrambled toward it, and Zacharias and Elias pulled her out. Adrian immediately whirled, pulling Nick out, just as the tunnel behind him completely caved in. Adrian dragged Nick out with such force that they both fell backward, with Nick landing on top of her.

Their eyes locked, and Nick gave her a grin. "Just another day in the life."

She smiled, relief filling her. *I love this man.* The thought came suddenly and out of nowhere, causing Adrian's already pounding heartbeat to falter in her chest.

Nick shifted and helped her up. She made no move to remove her hand. It felt right where it was.

"Guys," Myia said. She was looking at their interlocked hands, her lips twitching with amusement. "Don't forget about the rest of us. I'm very glad you weren't buried alive in that tunnel—but did you find anything? Was the near-death experience worth it?"

Adrian reached into her pocket, taking out her phone. She opened up her photos, taking in the petroglyphs.

"It most certainly was," she said.

Alcudia, Mallorca
4:15 P.M.

"I've never seen anything like this," Elias murmured, taking in the arrangement of petroglyphs.

They'd returned to the villa, where Adrian shared the photos she'd taken of the petroglyphs with the others. They were now gathered around Zacharias' large computer monitor, studying them.

"What do you think these could mean?" Adrian asked. "Why are there bulls in two of them?"

"Bulls were a common motif in ancient religions. The sacred bull was symbolic of strength, prowess, male virility," Elias replied. "What they're doing in the center of two of these . . . it could be an ancient origin of the Minotaur myth. But I don't know. Like I said, I've never seen an arrangement like this."

"I have a crazy suggestion," Nick said after several moments of silence. "Sometimes Occam's razor is the way to go. What if this is a map of some kind?"

Adrian froze, studying the petroglyphs. The labyrinths did seem to be arranged in a particular order.

"OK," Myia said, leaning in closer and studying each individual petroglyph. "I see what you could mean. But a map of what?"

Zacharias leaned over and opened another tab on his computer, pulling up a map of the Mediterranean. "Maybe of the Balearic Islands themselves?"

"No, it doesn't match the arrangement here. Besides, there are over a hundred islands in the Balearic Islands chain, and four main islands. There are twelve of these petroglyphs," Elias said.

Zacharias zoomed in on various areas of the map, looking at islands all around the Mediterranean, even moving eastward to the Aegean, but nothing seemed to correspond with the arrangement of the petroglyphs.

"Well, what if it's not a map—what if it's a representation of the stars or something?" Zacharias asked. "Elias, you mentioned the talaiots could also be astronomical observatories as well."

"Or this arrangement could just be religious symbolism and have nothing to do with Atlantis," Myia said with a heavy sigh of frustration.

But Adrian shook her head, studying the labyrinths. She had the feeling there was some meaning in the arrangement of the labyrinths, something that linked to Atlantis, just as there had been meaning to the arrangement of the peak sanctuaries and well temples that had ultimately led them here.

"No. I think there's something to this," Elias said, echoing her thoughts. "The arrangement seems very specific."

Adrian glanced over at Zacharias. She had wanted to loop in the team in DC ever since they'd boarded the flight to Palma, but Zacharias had refused, not wanting to open any lines of communication until they heard from his father. Adrian had insisted that their communication to Briggs was secure and hadn't been intercepted, but Zacharias hadn't budged. They'd ultimately agreed to hold off on contacting Briggs.

"I think now's the time to loop in our task force back in DC," she said firmly.

Zacharias looked as if he were going to protest when a piercing alarm interrupted him. He was instantly on his feet. He took out his phone, his face going pale.

"That's the security alarm. The villa's been breached." He turned to face them. "Leave through the back—there are woods behind here. A half mile out there's a road. I'll do my best to hold them off. Go. Now!"

They obliged, turning to race out of the study. But as soon as they made their way out to the hallway, several men were already inside, charging toward them, weapons raised.

Adrian and the others whirled, but a man and a woman—the tall, striking woman she recognized from Miletus—approached them from the opposite end of the hall.

They were trapped.

"Adrian West."

Adrian stilled as the darkly handsome man she recognized from Miletus emerged from behind the man and woman, giving her a frosty smile. "Stephanos Keliades. It's a pleasure to finally meet you in the flesh."

He approached her. Nick moved to stand protectively in front of her, but one of Stephanos' men grabbed him, pulling him back. Stephanos calmly lifted his pistol, slamming it down on her head, and her world went black.

CHAPTER 42

Unknown
7:37 P.M.

Adrian slowly came to, her temple throbbing as she took in her surroundings. For several moments, she blinked up at the ceiling, which appeared to . . . sway.

She looked around. She was lying on a bed in what appeared to be the cabin of a boat, complete with a small desk, chair, and a small window that looked out to the sea.

Adrian sat up abruptly. Grimacing, she rubbed her head where Stephanos had struck her. She ignored the pain, focusing. She was on a boat. Where were Nick and the others? Where was she now?

Panic coursing through her, she stumbled to her feet, looking around the cabin for anything she could use as a weapon, when the door swung open.

She stilled. Stephanos stood in the open doorway, a warm smile on his face, as if she were a guest, and he was the friendly host.

"How are you feeling?" he asked, giving her a regretful look. "I'm sorry I had to strike you, but your reputation precedes you."

"Where are the others?" she demanded.

"Alive, for now," Stephanos said with a casual shrug. "Their continued survivability depends on your cooperation."

"I want to see them."

"Of course," he said with a warm smile. He turned and made his way down the corridor, leaving the door open behind him. Adrian eyed his retreating back, heart hammering. If she moved quickly enough, she could strike.

But as soon as she stepped out of the cabin, two large guards stepped forward, one of them pressing a gun into the small of her back. They had been standing just outside the cabin, out of sight.

Up ahead, Stephanos glanced over his shoulder with a smirk, as if he'd read her mind and knew what she'd intended to do. Quelling her anger, Adrian trailed him down the corridor. By the surroundings, they appeared to be on a yacht. She passed several other cabins on her way down the corridor, but she couldn't see anything through their small windows.

Stephanos headed up a set of stairs and down another corridor, leading her into a room with large bay windows that overlooked the sea. Relief filled her at the sight of Nick and the others; even Dmitris, his face severely bruised, and Zacharias were there. But their hands and ankles were bound with zip ties, seated next to each other on a row of chairs, a guard on either side, weapons raised.

Elias was the only one separated from the group. He was seated in front of a long table in the center of the room, a map spread out in front of him, along with photographs of the petroglyphs. His hands and ankles were also bound, and there was another guard at his side, the tall woman she recognized from the Miletus site. Elias' face was pale with fear as he looked up to give her a subtle nod.

"The map in front of our friend Elias is of the Mediterranean," Stephanos said. "We've studied the petroglyphs you found—thank you for that, by the way—and my expert has concluded that it's likely a map. You and Elias are going to help us determine what it's pointing to, which we assume, of course, is Atlantis."

Stephanos turned, nodding to a woman whom Adrian hadn't noticed before. She sat in the corner in front of a laptop. She tapped her keyboard, and a screen descended from the ceiling. The screen displayed photographs of the petroglyphs, along with a map of the Mediterranean.

"Ticktock," Stephanos said. "I'm not a patient man. And if you try to mislead me, I will happily kill all of your friends. Two at a time. Starting with your boyfriend, of course."

Adrian swallowed hard as Stephanos gave her an icy smile. She didn't know exactly where they were or how to get them all out of this. They needed to get on the move, which would increase their chance of escaping. And that meant she needed to do what Stephanos asked. Given their predicament, she had no other choice.

The guard at her back nudged her forward, and Adrian took a seat next to Elias.

"We've been trying to figure out which landmasses these equate to. We just haven't been able to determine which ones," Elias said, his voice shaky. She could tell he was terrified, but trying to concentrate.

"We've been looking at all the islands in the region, even larger landmasses, to no avail," Stephanos added.

Adrian looked down at the petroglyphs and then at the map. She wondered if they were looking at this wrong.

She stood. As soon as she did, two guards immediately whirled to face her, their pistols aimed at her chest. Her heart rate increased, but she kept her tone steady. "I want to look at the petroglyphs from another angle."

"It's OK," Stephanos said to the two guards. "But if she makes one wrong move, shoot her boyfriend in the head, and then shoot Myia. Hell, shoot Zacharias as well. He just ... annoys me."

The men nodded, one keeping his pistol trained on her, while the other trained his weapon on Nick. Fear slithered through her, but she kept her focus, looking down at the photos of the petroglyphs and then the map. She recalled what she knew of Plato's writings about Atlantis' location. He'd referred to the Pillars of Hercules, the ancient term for the Strait of Gibraltar.

Adrian looked up at the map of the Mediterranean on the screen. "Zoom out," she said.

The woman obliged, zooming out. The map now showed Europe, the Atlantic, and northern Africa. Adrian moved closer to the screen, Stephanos' guards carefully tracking her movements. Her gaze flew over the island chains beyond the Strait of Gibraltar.

"We've already looked at island chains beyond the strait," Stephanos said, his tone sharpening with annoyance and impatience. "The Azores, the Madeira, the Canary Islands . . ."

"Zoom out more," Adrian said, ignoring him. The woman obliged. "Stop," she said abruptly.

Her eyes strayed to another island chain, one just off the western coast of Africa. The Cape Verde islands.

Heart hammering, Adrian glanced at the petroglyphs and back at the island chain. Cape Verde had ten main islands, while there were twelve petroglyphs. Still, she was encouraged.

"Try different arrangements of the petroglyphs over the Cape Verde islands to see if you come up with a match," Adrian said.

They all watched as the woman obliged, digitally transposing the petroglyphs over the Cape Verde islands in multiple arrangements until ten of the petroglyphs settled almost perfectly over the ten main islands. The other two petroglyphs were slightly to the north of the islands.

"Those other two petroglyphs, with the depictions of the sacred bull?" Stephanos asked.

"I think they correspond to two islands that were once there but sank into the sea," Adrian said, turning to meet his eyes. "Atlantis."

The room fell silent. Adrian thought of the peak sanctuaries on Crete, the well temples and nuraghes on Sardinia, the talaiots in the Balearics. They were directional waypoints, migration patterns, from an ancient, shared memory, tracing their migration in waves from a common point of origin.

Stephanos moved forward, pressing his hands over the two petroglyphs to the north of the Cape Verde island chain, his face reverent with awe. He stood there for a long moment before turning to one of his men.

"Get my plane ready," he ordered. "Me and my guests are taking a field trip."

CHAPTER 43

Atlantic Glider
North Atlantic Ocean
4:37 A.M.

The *Atlantic Glider* was a luxury yacht with facilities specifically designed for deep scuba diving. The yacht itself had a dozen cabins, a swimming pool, a spa and even a helideck. The dive shop held extensive scuba equipment: wet suits, fins, tanks, compressors, and oxygen generators. The crew had worked for Stephanos and other leaders of CHSR before, and they were paid handsomely to keep quiet about what they witnessed aboard.

Adrian and the others had flown on Stephanos' private plane from Palma de Mallorca Airport to Cesária Évora International Airport on the island of Sao Vicente in Cape Verde, where they'd boarded the chartered yacht at the port.

During the flight, Adrian was kept apart from Nick and the others, seated with Stephanos, the woman, Irina, and a guard, while Nick and the others were seated on the opposite end of the plane, next to another armed man. She'd hoped there would be a chance to escape during the journey, but Stephanos' men stayed on them at all times, keeping them bound and separate, never giving them an opportunity to break free.

Even on the *Atlantic Glider* they were kept apart. Adrian only got a glimpse of Nick and the others as their guards forced them onto the yacht at gunpoint before they disappeared into one of the cabins. Adrian and Elias were taken to the lower decks of the yacht, where they were outfitted in scuba diving gear.

From what Adrian had overheard during the flight, Stephanos' experts had worked fast once they'd pinpointed the ocean north of the Cape Verde islands as the potential location for Atlantis, pinpointing several areas to explore, using data from existing bathymetric surveys. Stephanos intended to use additional technology to explore the ocean's depths such as Lidar, an advanced method of scanning beneath the ocean's surface, and remote-sensing devices, but it took time to obtain and execute those resources. Since time was of the essence, he was going to dive to the potential site of the Atlantis ruins. Irina, two expert divers who worked for him, along with Adrian and Elias, were to make the dive as well.

"If either of you makes any attempt to sabotage me, I can send a signal to my men from the deep to shoot your friends. Don't test me," Stephanos warned.

Now, Adrian's heart hammered as she looked out over the deck to the deep waters of the Atlantic. She was out in the middle of the ocean and had no idea how they were going to get out of this. If the ruins of Atlantis were beneath the waters, Stephanos would no longer have any use for them. By the grim, terrified look on Elias' face, she knew he was aware of this as well.

Stephanos made Adrian and Elias dive first, followed by Stephanos, Irina and his two divers. As they dove beneath the waters, Adrian and Elias turned on their underwater torches to guide their way. She willed herself to calm down, concentrating on her breathing. The last time she had dived, it was to Cleopatra's underwater palace, and then, like now, despite the predicament they were in, she found a calm in the depths. The waters around them were murky, barely lit by their underwater torches, yet still soothing. She willed this calm to flow through her veins. She needed to think of a plan to save herself, Nick and the others once Stephanos found what he wanted.

Adrian could feel the pressure in her ears building as they continued to descend farther. Soon, she dimly heard commotion above them, coming from the yacht, drawing her attention up toward the surface. She wasn't certain, but it vaguely sounded like gunshots. Her heart leapt into her throat. Could someone have come to their rescue? Had Briggs and the team in DC tracked them here?

She looked over and saw Stephanos signaling to Irina and his divers, fearing that he was telling them to go back up, or to do away with them now. Instead, they just increased their rate of descent. She realized that Stephanos was determined to get to Atlantis, no matter what the cost.

They continued to descend, their underwater torches guiding their way. Adrian wondered what Stephanos would do if Atlantis wasn't here. If the commotion above wasn't a rescue, she wondered if he'd start killing them off, one by one . . . beginning with Nick. Fear surged through her at the thought, but she pushed it aside, forcing herself to focus on the task at hand—staying alive.

They continued to swim farther down, and she felt the increasing pressure of the waters above on her body. She wondered how much deeper they could safely go.

As soon as she had the thought, she spotted something below.

Adrian's pulse rate accelerated. Stephanos' divers shone their backup lights down into the depths, speeding up their descent. Stephanos, Irina, Adrian, and Elias were right behind them.

If she could have gasped, she would have.

Farther below them, in the depths, she could

see the ruins of a submerged city, the crumbling remains of walls, buildings, statues, pillars—even paved streets.

They had found Atlantis.

CHAPTER 44

Atlantic Glider
North Atlantic Ocean
5:02 A.M.

Nick tensed as he heard shouts and gunfire outside on the deck.

He was in a cabin with Myia; he suspected Dmitris and Zacharias were in another cabin. A sour-faced armed guard, whom Nick had silently nicknamed Sour Face, was in the room with them, but he stiffened at the sound of gunfire. The guard hesitated, glancing back and forth between his prisoners and the chaos outside.

"I'd check that out if I were you," Nick said drily.

"Shut up," Sour Face snarled, but he still looked hesitant. As the gunfire grew closer, he seemed to make his decision, leaving the cabin and locking it behind him.

"I thought he'd never leave," Myia said. "Who do you think that is?"

"For our sake, I hope it's the good guys," Nick said.

He grunted with effort as he stood on his bound legs, crashing the chair he was in several times into the wall behind him until it disintegrated.

It took some work, but with some wriggling, he undid the ties on his wrists. He quickly bent down to yank off the ties around his ankles before he turned to Myia, freeing her from her chair and ties.

They looked around the room—there was nothing to use as a weapon. Nick reached for the discarded arms of his destroyed chair. Myia raised her eyebrows.

"Hey, it's better than nothing," he muttered.

Myia took the other arm, and together they moved to the cabin door. They unlocked it, but it was blocked from the outside. Sour Face had pushed a chair or something against it. Together, Nick and Myia slammed their bodies against the door until whatever was blocking it became dislodged.

Nick pushed open the door, taking a cautious step out.

"Hey!"

Nick whirled. Sour Face raced toward them, his expression tight with fury. He raised his weapon to fire.

Nick stumbled back into the cabin, dragging Myia behind him, slamming the door and locking it. Sour Face fired two shots at the doorknob, causing it to fall off. The door partially opened.

Nick clutched the arm of the chair—Sour Face was only seconds away from entering. He turned to look at Myia, who gave him a nod, understanding what he intended to do.

The door burst open, and Sour Face entered, gun raised, but Nick and Myia were ready. Nick hit him on the side of his temple as hard as he could. As he pitched forward, Nick grabbed his gun while Myia dealt Sour Face another blow to the head, knocking him out cold.

"Those chair arms aren't seeming so bad as weapons now, are they?" Nick asked, gesturing at the knocked-out guard on the floor.

Myia just smiled and rolled her eyes. They darted out of the room, Nick clutching the gun, knocking and shouting at each cabin door they passed for Dmitris and Zacharias, but there was no answer. But he kept going; he needed to get to the upper decks, to find out what was going on, to get to Adrian. Adrian, who was trapped with a madman hundreds of feet underwater. The thought of his partner made him pick up his pace.

As they reached the stairs that led to the upper decks, he froze at the sound of footsteps descending.

"Get behind me!" he shouted at Myia, getting into a defensive stance and raising his weapon.

The half-dozen men and women who were descending, wore uniforms of the Cape Verde

Maritime Police. Relief washed over him. *The good guys.*

But they were looking at him like he was the enemy, shouting at him in Portuguese to drop his weapon.

He complied, raising his hands, and getting to his knees. "My name is Nick Harper! I'm an American federal agent with the FBI!"

The police still approached him with weapons raised, though they paused as a familiar face moved past them, stepping forward.

It was Athena Karras. She turned to the police, shouting at them in Portuguese to stand down. She hurried forward, helping him and Myia to their feet.

"It's good to see you, Nick," she said. "Where's Adrian?"

"She's still in danger," he said, his heart hammering. "She's hundreds of feet underwater with Stephanos Keliades."

CHAPTER 45

North Atlantic Ocean
5:23 A.M.

Adrian took in the ruins below. A part of her still couldn't believe what she was seeing. This was *Atlantis*. The mythological, advanced civilization that sank beneath the sea.

But here it was, right before her eyes . . . a myth come to life. A once bustling city that predated even the ancient Minoan civilization by thousands of years.

She could see the crumbling paved stones of what had once been roads; pillars that had once held up grand structures, statues of ancient, unknown gods; dilapidated remains of buildings that had once been houses, temples, warehouses.

Stephanos, Irina, and his two divers dove deeper, moving even closer to the ruins. Amazement filled her when she saw exactly what they were swimming toward.

The ruins of a labyrinth, made up of disintegrating stones, lying between the foundations of what had once been buildings, possibly temples.

Elias started to dive after Stephanos, but she reached out her arm to stop him, gripping his arm. He looked at her, and she held up her hand, indicating for him to wait. She then pointed to the center of the labyrinth.

A realization had dawned as she'd watched Stephanos swim toward it, a recollection of another meaning of the center of the labyrinth. The minotaur in the center of the Cretan labyrinth. The bulls in the center of the two labyrinths that represented Atlantis. Now she realized what they could also represent.

Danger.

Elias seemed to understand and remained where he was. They hovered, floating in the depths, watching as Stephanos and the others drew closer and closer to the labyrinth's center, hoping that she was right.

STEPHANOS TOOK in the wonder of the ruins of the city beneath him ... Atlantis.

A swelling of emotion filled him as he descended closer to the labyrinth, the symbol that had helped guide him here. Somewhere within these ruins, he would find the secrets of that ancient weapon of Greek fire, the key to the destruction that lay ahead . . . and then the inevitable rebirth. *The ancient wisdom.*

He was not a religious man, not even worshiping the old gods as many members of the *Archaia Sofia* did, but now he uttered a prayer to all the supernatural entities he could think of. He wished his father were here with him, to see the greatness of Atlantis for his own eyes.

Elation coursed through him as he drew closer to the center of the labyrinth. To his amazement, he saw several levers attached to the crumbling stone walls that made up the heart of the labyrinth. They had long since rusted over, but he imagined in their time that they were made of pure gold.

Stephanos, Irina, and the other two divers moved closer to the levers. Stephanos reached out to one, hungry to know what pulling it would reveal. More of the ancient city? Treasure? A cache of ancient weapons?

Next to him, his expert divers were making hand signals indicating caution. Stephanos ignored them. He'd been working most of his life to get to this moment; he wasn't going to wait a moment longer.

He turned, meeting Irina's eyes. She smiled, the same smile she'd given him when they'd taken the papyrus. He returned it, glad that he'd brought her with him, his previous irritation with her a distant memory. She could appreciate this moment almost as much as he did.

With great effort and using all of his strength, Stephanos pulled the lever, anticipation flooding every part of his body. Pulling the lever revealed an opening from which flames shot out, and a rumbling from within the walls of the labyrinth began to shake the seabed below.

Agonizing pain seared Stephanos' flesh, and he dimly realized that he was on fire.

As the earth beneath him trembled, and more flames erupted from the walls of the labyrinth, consuming him, Irina, and his divers from the deep, his last sight was of the ruins of Atlantis around him.

Adrian and Elias had already begun their ascent, careful to monitor their speed to avoid decompression sickness.

She heard the rumbling below, and panic rippled through her. They couldn't ascend too rapidly, the nitrogen in their bodies was expanding during their ascent. Increasing their speed would only endanger them and possibly be fatal—they needed time to expel the excess nitrogen from their bodies.

She could feel the pressure from the explosion beneath, and her panic rose. She and Elias kicked up, slightly picking up their speed. They couldn't ascend more than sixty feet per minute. They were at fifty feet per minute now. But she didn't know how far the effects of the underwater explosion would reach, or if it were to suck them back down . . .

Focus. Adrian continued to kick up. She could see the sky above the surface. Close, so close. The rumbling increased, and she felt the force of it on her body, threatening to tug her back down.

Adrian kicked, now pushing herself to the maximum ascent speed, with Elias following suit. She was almost there. And just as the force from the underwater explosion increased—

Two strong arms reached beneath the surface of the water, pulling her out.

It was Nick, his face wild with relief as he helped her onto the deck. Next to her, two maritime police pulled Elias onto the deck as well. The effect of the underwater explosion was mild on the surface, with only a slight rippling of the waves and rocking of the yacht to show its effect.

Adrian met Nick's eyes, and he leaned forward, capturing her lips with his. Adrian returned his kiss, all of her feelings for him bubbling to the surface, from years past and the last few months: a catharsis, and a feeling of what those ancient peoples had sought when they searched for Atlantis. Home.

CHAPTER 46

Ponta do Sol, Cape Verde
2:49 P.M.

Adrian sat next to Nick, Myia and Elias on the deck of the police boat, which was docked at the port of Ponta do Sol. The police divers had taken preliminary photos of the Atlantis site, and they were studying them on a tablet that belonged to one of the maritime police officers.

The maritime police had cordoned off the waters around the underwater ruins for both safety reasons after the underwater explosion, and to prepare it for the extensive surveying it was to undergo by both scientists and underwater archaeologists.

The police had also taken Stephanos' surviving men, and the crew aboard the yacht into custody. Adrian, Nick, and the others had spent the last several hours being interviewed by Athena and the local police; the police were still interviewing Dmitris and Zacharias inside one of the cabins.

"How did you find us?" Adrian had asked Athena.

"A police lieutenant who was actually working for Stephanos and CHSR," Athena replied. She offered Adrian a pained smile. "He took me hostage and tried to kill me, but that's a story for another day."

Athena told her that once they linked Stephanos to this lieutenant, her boss had their cyber unit run a full background on him, including financial. Stephanos used multiple aliases, and they found that one of those aliases had made a large financial transfer to a private yacht company that leased the *Atlantic Glider* to him. Once they tracked the *Atlantic Glider*'s course from the Cape Verde Coast Guard, they'd immediately left Athens to head to Cape Verde, looping in the maritime police.

"We're investigating Stephanos' operations—of which there are many—from bioterrorism to illegal weapons. We're also investigating CHSR, which was a front for much of his activities. Stephanos was trying to facilitate a nuclear war through any means necessary. It'll take time for us to unravel everything he was planning. We're still interviewing, tracking, and arresting his associates," Athena continued.

The police divers were still investigating the underwater explosion, which looked like a cache of

Greek fire, stored in the walls of the labyrinth, caused it. Stephanos must have activated it by pulling the lever, an ancient ignition device. The deadly chemical cocktail of Greek fire had sat there for millennia. They also believed, from a preliminary survey of the site, that a series of violent earthquakes had caused the ancient city to sink beneath the waters, just as Plato had written.

"A fail-safe," Adrian said, looking at Nick and the others. "It's another meaning of the center of the labyrinth, going back even further than the minotaur. The labyrinth petroglyphs we found on Mallorca even had bulls in the center. I think they were not only a representation of Atlantis' strength, but a warning and representation of danger, something true descendants of the Atlanteans would know. The ancient wisdom Stephanos and his secret society was obsessed with . . . I wonder if it was this fail-safe all along."

"The Atlanteans must have implemented it before the city sank beneath the sea, to protect it from falling into the wrong hands," Elias mused.

After they spoke to the police, Adrian and Nick briefly spoke to Briggs and updated him, though they would have to give him a full debriefing once they returned to DC.

"I can't believe it," Myia said now, taking in the photos of the site. "When I first heard about there being a historical Atlantis, I was skeptical. But here it is."

"Here it is," Adrian echoed, her eyes roaming

over the ruins of the ancient structures lying beneath the waves.

The explosion had only directly affected the labyrinth and slightly damaged the ruins of some of the nearby buildings, but most of the ruins remained.

Adrian stood, moving to the railing of the boat and looking off into the distance, toward the site; multiple ships and helicopters were making their way toward it. Nick joined her, taking her hand, and they stood in silence. There had been a shift between them since their kiss—a positive one. Adrian no longer had to hide her feelings for him. She no longer wanted to. She knew they would talk more about the change in their relationship once they returned home.

Her thoughts returned to Atlantis. Adrian imagined the magnitude of what it must have been like in its heyday, before the violent earthquakes that sank it deep beneath the ocean, sending its inhabitants to seek new homes. They would populate the islands of the Mediterranean, building replicas of their ancient civilization over time. They'd left clues in their labyrinth petroglyphs, their sanctuaries, their temples . . . from their collective shared memory, a path back to their lost home.

CHAPTER 47

One Week Later
FBI Headquarters
Washington, DC
11:34 A.M.

The man watched Adrian from a distance as she entered FBI Headquarters with her partner at her side, pride swelling in his heart. It had pained him to stay away, to watch her from afar, but it was the sacrifice he'd made so that she could be safe and live a full life. He was so proud of her achievements and what she had made of herself. Despite the pain it had caused him, he knew it was worth it for that reason alone.

But now, all that had to come to an end. Her recent successes had put a target on her back, and she was once again in danger. He had no choice but to emerge from the shadows again, if only to protect her. His heart tightened as he let his gaze roam over her once more before turning to fade into the crowds.

He'd already set the wheels in motion. It was up to her to follow the path . . . to the key.

∼

Washington, DC
6:42 P.M.

ADRIAN AND NICK headed down her building's corridor to her apartment after yet another debrief meeting. They'd had to sum up their experiences several times to several different departments, including their task force. Briggs assured them they were done with debriefs—for now.

The police had recovered Solon's papyrus from Stephanos' property, and news of Atlantis' discovery had finally been released to the public. At their request, she and Nick had been left out of the noise of the discovery, and the focus was on the find itself. Teams of historians, scientists, and underwater archaeologists had descended upon Cape Verde, and the area around the site was now protected, with all manner of advanced technologies, from Lidar to sonar to remote-sensing devices being used to fully map out the site.

Elias was back at work at the National Archaeological Museum. As soon as he'd returned to Athens, he'd married his fiancée. He'd told Adrian and Nick over the phone that he'd realized how short and precious life was, and he didn't want to wait another minute to marry the love of his life.

Myia had gone underground, to return to her previous life of restoring artifacts to their home countries, but not before giving Adrian her actual email address.

"I've maybe taken a liking to you, West," Myia had told her with a grin. Myia had also confirmed that her name was not an alias but her true name. Her mother had a love for ancient Greek philosophers.

Athena had been promoted and was getting recognition for her work on the case; she was now leading the investigation into Stephanos' operations and into CHSR, which had been disbanded and was undergoing multiple investigations for criminal ties. Athena had also linked former Lieutenant Tobias Vasileiou to her partner Stavros' death; he was currently in prison awaiting trial for his murder and a multitude of other crimes. She'd even reopened the case of Myia's mother's death at Adrian's request.

As for Adrian and Nick, their relationship had shifted with ease to a romantic one, which Adrian realized was just friendship set on fire. Nick had told her what he'd intended to tell her, on the flight to Palma, that they one day take a vacation there when they had a break.

"A break?" she'd asked skeptically, and he laughed.

"A break. One of these days," Nick replied.

"I think we can make it work," she agreed. "Let's just try to not get almost buried alive this time."

"Deal."

They were now walking hand in hand to her apartment to cook dinner and stay in and talk about "non saving the world things," at Nick's request. Briggs had even ordered them to take at least a few days off before returning to the bureau. The old workaholic Adrian would have resisted, but now she was looking forward to spending time with Nick.

They reached her apartment, and Adrian halted at the sight of an envelope partially slipped under her door. She exchanged an uneasy glance with Nick, reaching for her service weapon before picking up the envelope and unlocking the door.

She and Nick entered, their weapons at the ready, scanning the apartment for any sign of an intruder. But it was empty.

Shaking, Adrian opened the envelope, revealing a single piece of paper with a series of letters typed in the center.

EYKGFLANITOYTCIVOYKESEHEYI

ISLENHIWTIHE

"Let me guess," Nick said with a heavy sigh. "Some sort of code."

"It looks like an anagram," Adrian said slowly, studying the letters.

She sat down on her couch, taking out a legal pad, and together she and Nick worked to unscramble the words, until they eventually found the solution.

THE KEY YOU SEEK LIES WITHIN THE FLOATING CITY

"The floating city?" Nick asked with a frown.

Adrian met his eyes, her heartbeat picking up its pace. "Venice."

∼

THE ADVENTURE CONTINUES in Book Four, THE VENETIAN KEY. *Start reading now!*

THE VENETIAN KEY

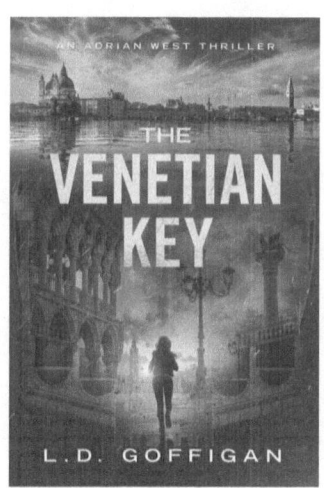

An earth-shattering secret. A long-lost key. A lethal pursuit...

After a cryptic letter summons Adrian West and Nick Harper to Venice, a revelation from the past shatters Adrian's world...

They must pick up the pieces to follow a trail of

cryptic clues, unraveling the threads of a conspiracy rooted deep in Venetian history.

In a desperate race from the canals of Venice, the ancient streets of Dubrovnik, to the Byzantine-era relics of Istanbul, Adrian and Nick must prevent a clandestine society from carrying out a lethal, centuries-old agenda that could spell humanity's extinction...

Start reading now!

AUTHOR'S NOTE

Atlantis has inspired our collective imagination for centuries. I've always found Atlantis compelling, and was intrigued by the notion of a historical one. What would a historical Atlantis look like, if it existed? That was the starting point for Adrian's latest adventure.

The only mention of Atlantis we currently have is from Plato's dialogues *Timaeus* and *Critias*. If a historical Atlantis were to exist, the first thing we'd need is another verifiable historical mention—hence, Solon's papyrus, my invention for the purposes of this novel.

Solon was a real person, an Athenian statesman mentioned by Plato in his writings about Atlantis.

Linear A and Cretan hieroglyphs are real undeciphered writing systems from ancient Crete. And while Linear B, which has been deciphered since the 1950s, has been used to analyze Linear A, both writing systems remain undeciphered.

AUTHOR'S NOTE

Pre-Greek languages are fascinating, they are a language or languages spoken before the languages of the Indo-European family, from which many of the major world languages descend. Much about these languages are unknown and only theorized about, their existence fossilized in words of other languages. No known writing of these languages exist. The etymology of the word Atlantis is theorized by some linguists to have pre-Greek origins. I ran with this theory, giving it the pre-Greek name Atai, which I invented based on what little I know about the pre-Greek substrate.

As mentioned in the novel, there are the ruins of three Minoan palace complexes found on Crete today; I've had the pleasure of visiting Knossos, and it's truly magnificent in person. The Dikti Mountain range also exists, but the cave peak sanctuary they find, along with the labyrinth petroglyph, is my invention.

Peak sanctuaries, nuraghes, and well temples all exist, though the notion of ancient peoples using them as directional waypoints are my invention. (On that note, Ikaria island exists, but the peak sanctuary that points to Troy is also my invention).

The archaeological sites of Troy and Miletus exist, complete with the wooden horse near the entrance for visitors to see, as well as the layers marked out by the excavators of the different layers of Troy—including the Troy described by Homer. Miletus does have the connection to Crete that I mentioned in the novel (there is even a place called Miletus in Crete), but the labyrinth symbol found is my invention.

I had no idea how rich Sardinia's ancient culture was until I began my research for this novel. My characters were originally going to head right to Spain from Turkey, but there were too many juicy historical details in Sardinia for me to ignore. The labyrinth carved on the wall of the Luzzanas tomb, for example, exists and is pretty close to how I describe it, though I've not yet had the pleasure of visiting it. The well temple of Santa Cristina also exists as I describe it in the novel, though its directional waypoint status is my invention.

I've been to two of the Balearic islands on vacation, and it would be easy to dismiss them as mere party islands, but they do have an interesting and rich history, with their impressive Talaiotic culture. The Balearic island sites my characters visit all exist, though I invented the tunnel and embellished some of the ruins they find at Bocchoris, as well as the petroglyphs they find there. Elias' mention of labyrinth symbols found all over the islands is also my invention—the Talaiotic structures, however, do number in the hundreds.

The labyrinth is an ancient symbol that is surprisingly mysterious in origin. No one can definitely state what they symbolize, though there are an abundance of theories, many religious in nature. The connection in this novel of the labyrinth

AUTHOR'S NOTE

symbol to Atlantis is my invention, though the possible meanings match many of the theories out there.

CHSR is fictional, along with the secret society *Archaia Sofia,* though it is loosely based on the Greek research agency FORTH, the Foundation for Research and Technology.

Greek fire was an actual ancient weapon that existed, working to great effect for the Byzantines and other armies. The military did such a good job of hiding how it was made that its recipe remains a mystery to this day, though theories abound.

For the location of Atlantis, I chose the Cape Verde islands because of their relatively remote position in the North Atlantic Ocean and the volcanic nature of the islands themselves; it is certainly possible that one of these islands could sink beneath the ocean after a violent eruption or earthquake.

In my research for this novel, I read countless articles, research papers, and of course, books. A couple of the most helpful resources I used include *The Birth of Classical Europe* by Simon Price and Peter Thonemann, and *1177 B.C.: The Year Civilization Collapsed* by Eric H. Cline, which is an utterly fascinating read that I highly recommend, and eerily prescient for the modern world.

I hope you've enjoyed Adrian's latest adventure. Her adventure continues in one of the most fascinating cities in the world . . . Venice.

AUTHOR'S NOTE

Until next time,
—L.D.G.

2022

ABOUT THE AUTHOR

L.D. Goffigan writes fast-paced thrillers and action-adventure with historical intrigue. She studied film and dramatic writing at New York University and currently divides her time between France and California.

When not writing, you can find her traveling to places she's never been, reading the latest book which strikes her fancy, or watching a documentary about ancient mysteries.

To be notified about new releases, visit L.D. Goffigan's website to join her newsletter. Subscribers are also alerted to giveaways and exclusive bonus content.

Stay in touch!
ld@ldgoffiganbooks.com
ldgoffiganbooks.com

www.ingramcontent.com/pod-product-compliance
Lightning Source LLC
LaVergne TN
LVHW091720070526
838199LV00050B/2478